THE CHALLENGE
OF EVIL

THE CHALLENGE OF EVIL

Further Conversations with
Richard

Channeled by
Graham Bernard

DESTINY BOOKS
ROCHESTER, VERMONT

Destiny Books
One Park Street
Rochester, Vermont 05767

Library of Congress Cataloging-in-Publication Data

Bernard, Graham.
    The challenge of evil.

    1. Spirit writings. 2. Good and evil — Miscellanea.
I. Richard (Spirit) II. Title.
BF1301.B416   1988   133.9'3   88-3759
ISBN 0-89281-205-2

10 9 8 7 6 5 4 3 2 1

Destiny Books is a division of Inner Traditions International,
Ltd.

Typography by Royal Type
Text design and production by Studio 31
Printed and bound in the United States.

Distributed to the book trade in the United States by Harper
and Row Publishers, Inc.

Distributed to the book trade in Canada by Book Center,
Montreal, Quebec.

*To Teach,
for her constructive influence
upon me from both worlds.*

THE NEW SITUATION in the world (the ability to self-destruct) requires an equally new understanding of why you are where you are. The incarnate world was created for the specific purpose of allowing humanity to choose, of its own free will, between self-will and God's Will. This new situation you face requires a radically different understanding. Not only is your present life as well as the earth on which you live at stake, but the very plan of life itself.

Understanding that plan requires you to enlarge your concept of yourselves, to include not just your life on earth, but life when you are not on earth. To do this you must listen to those who have gone on.

R.

Contents

IV. An Overview

V. Reverberations

VI. The Practice of Faith

THE CHALLENGE
OF EVIL

Richard's Preface

In considering the meaning of our struggle with evil, we are principally concerned with responsibility. Human beings are responsible for the creation and proliferation of evil and are equally responsible for its elimination.

The balance of power in the world has definitely tipped toward deterrence and evil, and so it behooves all those who are dedicated to construction to do all in their power to at least restore the balance. In this way, God's plan for our redemption can function in accordance with His Will.

It will require the utmost effort of each of you to be able to alleviate the problems and acquire the necessary qualities to keep moving forward toward the ultimate goal, perfection. This is your primary responsibility, an intrinsic part of which is your responsibility for the welfare of those within your immediate sphere of influence. If this effort is not made, a period of darkness will most certainly descend, another Dark Age, which will play havoc with the earth and all its creatures.

Those who are dedicated to evil rejoice in the present state of affairs and, as the effort is made to right the balance, they will respond with all of the power of the Forces of Darkness. The great impending struggle, which is inevitable if the world is to be ruled by the Will of God, will engage the Forces of Light and the Forces of Darkness in conflict, each vying for the souls of the uncommitted. This struggle will permeate all elements of life. As is evidenced by the events of the world today, now is the time to choose in favor of the Forces of Light; now is the time to assume your rightful role in the world of construction so that God's Will can be done on earth through you.

This, then, is your responsibility. What you do about it is up to you.

Introduction
By Graham Bernard

Although our first book, *Why You Are Who You Are*, was channeled through me over a relatively short time span, it occurred only after my wife Madeleine and I had been in communication with Richard, our guide, for many years.

It was in 1964, after we had been introduced to the books of Stewart Edward White, that we started our first tentative efforts at communication. This led us to Richard, who guided us from the Ouija board, through automatic writing to what he called brain impingement, our present mode of communication. Brain impingement is the projection of Richard's thoughts on my brain, utilizing my vocabulary. It is his thoughts put into my words. The fundamental action of the recipient is to listen inwardly with a strong intention to hear.

Richard had been a close friend of mine before he was "accidentally" killed in World War II. As a young ensign he was standing guard on an aircraft carrier, when he was shot and killed by inadvertent gunfire from a landing plane.*

The information we received from Richard for most of those years was intended to help us understand life, and how it is to be lived, so we could grow according to plan. I found great difficulty in following such a plan.

---

* For a fuller account, see *Why You Are Who You Are*.

I kept slipping back into old compulsions that are deterrent to growth and development. All the while I kept feeling that there must be some purpose to Richard's insistence that I try to follow his rules, but I didn't have a clue as to what it might be. He had mentioned the possibility of a book or books coming out of our effort, but as time passed and I persisted in my old ways in spite of all, it didn't seem to me that we would ever do anything with the information we had.

Then suddenly I was struck with kidney failure and everything changed. Before I started the trauma of repeated hospitalizations, tests, surgery, and transfusions, Richard appeared to me, and the sight of that beatific apparition changed my life. This difficult time, which culminated in dialysis, lasted almost four years, during two years of which Richard gave me the particular material of our first book.

Why You Are Who You Are was to act as a primer, providing all of the essential ingredients of this teaching in brief concise form. All subsequent communications would be elements of the first teaching, each subject expanded into a book. Henceforth Madeleine and I would work together. She was to provide an outline for each book, and from the outline we were to receive the information Richard would give us, from which I was to compile a book, with Madeleine acting as editor. In this way we would each be doing what we do best, and we could manage a book in about a year, instead of the two years it had taken me on the first one. It was hoped we could finally achieve six books and perhaps more in the time remaining to us. Since Madeleine and I are both in our seventies, we are keeping our fingers crossed!

When Richard announced that the second book was to be about evil, I balked! We had covered the subject of deterrence (his term for all that deters spiritual growth), and its ultimate outcome evil, sufficiently already, and I couldn't face a whole book on this depressing subject. However, Richard prevailed and Madeleine subsequently received an outline from him that opened up the subject in such a way that it became apparent to us both that it was not only necessary to do this book, but it was essential.

Since the Crucial Concepts in the original book are to obtain throughout the entire scope of this teaching, it is necessary to re-state them here, with the addition of concepts we have learned since the original publication. It would be well to study and digest these before proceeding.

CRUCIAL CONCEPTS

1. **Immortality** is a reality.
2. **Reincarnation** is a fact.
3. The nature of **God's Being** is truth.
4. The nature of **God's Will** is construction, which leads to spiritual growth.
5. The nature of **God's Love** is harmony.
6. The nature of **self-will** is deterrence (all that deters spiritual growth).
7. **Deterrent Force** is the collective energy of all thought, action and emotion that deters spiritual progress.
8. **Constructive Force** is the collective energy of all thought, action, and emotion that contributes to spiritual progress.
9. **Frequency** (the number of vibrations per minute) is the barometer of development. The degree of frequency of all things, incarnate or discarnate, indicates the degree of spiritual growth.

10. The **Place of Self-Deception** is a state of frequency in which those who are unwilling and unable to see themselves clearly remain after death until and unless they can learn to see themselves as they truly are.

11. The **Place of Preparation** is the state of frequency in which we prepare for our next life. If we can see ourselves clearly, it becomes our "home".

12. The **Lower Regions** are a lower level of frequency in which those who are dedicated to evil find themselves after an incarnation.

13. The **Realms** are the level of frequency in which one finds oneself after one no longer needs to reincarnate. There are seven Realms to be achieved before perfection can be reached.

14. The **Purposes** — the seven purposes are elements of the Realms. Each Realm has a purpose that must be gained before one can move on.

15. The **elements of development** are the particular circumstances of an incarnation.

16. Our **spiritual equipment** (love, sense of truth, and intuition) is brought with us to earth from the Place of Preparation, to be used to cope with growth problems.

17. **Grace** is the ever-present opportunity to begin again, to start over.

18. The **quality–quantity** factor is basic to the functioning of an incarnation. Quality is earned in the discarnate world, but it cannot become permanent until it is given quantity in the living out of an incarnation in the incarnate world.

19. The **Law of Parallels** is an answering flow of energy from the discarnate world to all thoughts and acts from the incarnate world.

20. **Event** is the culmination of converging circumstances.
21. **Intent** is the plan of a life, which has been determined prior to reincarnation.
22. **Deterrants** are deterrent souls in the discarnate world.
23. **Thoughts are things.** Constructive thought contributes to construction as a force at large. Deterrent thought contributes to deterrence as a force at large.
24. **Self-possession** is possession of the temporal self by the eternal self: the ultimate state of humanity.

In response to Richard's request we put our minds to the subject of evil. As a result, we found our concern for the terrorism, killing, drug addiction, irresponsible relationships and just plain greed that is evident, not satisfactorily resolved. Richard decided to give us a deeper understanding of why this has come about and who is responsible. He wanted us to know also that there is a solution to all of the deterrence and evil that plague the world.

Richard asked for a question from us that could identify our deepest concerns and might act as a springboard for another informative conversation. What follows is the harvest of our efforts. The questions are ours — the answers are his.

I. Our Struggle with Evil

This great carnival of evil
has wrought havoc with all our
ethical preconceptions.

—Dietrich Bonhoeffer,
Letters from Prison—1945

The Balance of Power

Why is there so much evil in the World? (Richard answered by instructing me to draw this diagram:)

God's Will ◄──────── Free Will ────────► Self Will
(Construction)   (Deterrence)

If free will chooses self-will it becomes deterrent; it deters God's Will. Persistent deterrence, resulting in a limitation of the functioning of God's Will on earth, becomes evil. That is why those factors, which influence the development of humanity must at least be kept in balance both within the individual and in society as a whole.

What will happen if they are not?

If the present situation gains sufficient momentum (and it appears to be doing just that) the result will bring on a period of darkness for mankind in which spiritual growth is deterred world-wide, another Dark Age. Although periods of darkness and renascence are characteristic of life on earth, because of reincarnation the restorative powers are always rejuvenated, however gradually. The danger of greater and more prolonged calamity increases as the power with which humanity has been entrusted also increases. It is therefore extremely important for all constructive souls to do their utmost

11

now, so the freedom of individuals to progress is not curtailed further by Deterrent Force. The problem increases as those who have succumbed to Deterrent Force gain more and more control. When this happens, those in both the incarnate and discarnate worlds who cannot withstand them are sucked into a negative vortex from which they may recover, but only after a very long period of time. Each uncommitted soul affects the balance of power.

Do you mean the balance of power will inevitably be restored?

Fundamental to the plan of reincarnation is preparation that enables those who return to fulfill a constructive and needed purpose. There are also those who no longer need to reincarnate, but choose to come back for the sake of humankind. Their lives encourage and give direction to others. In the perspective of history we see what they have done to restore the balance of power. We also look forward intuitively to their coming again, the "second coming." If you stop to consider, you'll agree that the future without great souls is unthinkable.

What do you mean by the "second coming"?

The "second coming" is the promise. God Himself will sacrifice Himself again and again, if need be, to save not only those who are already His, but all the lost sheep. God's Will cannot be destroyed. Remember this!

Then we needn't fear ultimately, since the balance will be restored no matter what we do. Each individual contribution doesn't really make that much difference.

You're wrong. Each individual contribution does make a difference. It makes a difference in human misery and suffering, in devastation and ugliness, in waste, in a ruined earth and lost art. The list is endless. Instead of growing and expanding and loving, humanity is shrinking and contracting and hating!

What can we do to turn things around?

First there must be realization of the untoward possibilities that this situation presents, and then, most importantly, all of you on the side of construction must assume responsibility for yourselves, your thoughts, your acts, and your reactions to other people and to events.

What exactly is this struggle about?

God's Will (construction) versus self-will (deterrence) is the basis for the struggle for domination of the incarnate world. The condition of the whole is dependent upon the condition of each. It's your choice. You are free to choose your own way, but the balance can be maintained only if enough of you choose the way of construction and guard your intentions with persistent vigilance.

As our knowledge and powers seem to have outstripped our capacity to handle them, aren't the odds stacked against us?

Don't forget that knowledge and powers can be used for construction as well as deterrence. This is exactly what can happen if all people do their utmost to fulfill the goal that they have come to achieve. This could right the balance again.

We wish you to understand that the least you can do is maintain the balance of power within yourself. Obviously the most desirable outcome is to be able to tip the scale altogether toward God's Will, but that cannot be a consideration in ordinary life as it has developed. It takes a great deal of effort and development to tip the scale even slightly toward God's Will. It takes no effort to tip it toward self-will. Therefore, both for the individual and for the world, it is essential to understand the importance of maintaining enough control to prevent rapid deterioration, to understand the value of effort, and to try to gain enough mastery slowly but surely to add strength and power on the side of God's Will. This is of the utmost urgency, now that the scale has tipped toward deterrence.

Why is this so?

Materialism is a strong feature of life today, because so many of you have forgotten your role in God's dream of spiritual perfection. Once deterrence sets in, no matter at what level or in what category, spiritual values are lost. This is true whether we are discussing materialism, or lack of consideration for others — the poor, the neglected, the ill — or the misuse of all the scientific advancements which proliferate today.

You would think that with these recent advancements in scientific discoveries and achievements, a reverence for creation would follow, but not so. With all of our knowledge, we still can kill each other over differing attitudes of mind, often in a misguided concern for right. What we believe affects how we act, and pride generated by self-will fosters much of what we choose to adhere to.

How would you characterize the present situation?

It is precarious indeed.

As the population grows, so grows the intent of deterrence. Construction is losing the struggle for the balance of power! All possible avenues of constructive effort must be utilized in order to try to regain balance! The ultimate goal of God's dream requires that the balance of power become completely constructive. Therefore, you who seek God's Will must realize the danger you are facing at present.

Deterrants (deterrent souls in the discarnate world) are doing all in their power to manipulate those who remain uncommitted. Even those who are committed to construction could be influenced by deterrence in just one unguarded moment. Deterrants make their gains by attacking karmic problems with Deterrent Force.

Are you really saying that discarnates actually intervene in our lives by attacking our karmic problems with Deterrent Force?
Yes.

Please explain that.
This is a subject I will deal with at greater length later. First let's concentrate on examples of the problem as you see it on earth. Those who are never sure of themselves, who suffer from hallucinations and aberrant behavior, are vulnerable to Deterrent Force. They in turn use others to satisfy their uncontrollable needs. People need people, but this situation is thrown completely out of balance when we find that people use, misuse, and abuse others for their own satisfaction, and, in the process, damage both themselves and their victims. This results not only in broken hearts and bodies, but also in broken spirits.

For instance, a disease that becomes uncontrollable as a result of detterence must, once activated, follow its own laws whether they lead to the innocent or to the guilty. If science overcomes one such disease, another will arise, because it is the physical parallel of a spiritual condition. The point to be examined is not so much whether sex is physically safe as whether it is spiritually safe. Is it motivated by love or self-indulgence?

Whether or not it leads to disease, promiscuity has its karma. The function of moral law is infallible. A complete change of sexual behavior toward love and responsibility must be achieved before God's Will can be done.

What about the innocent victims, whether they are adult, or even children? Why should they suffer?

As this conversation continues, I hope that we will develop an understanding of this. No sense can be made of seemingly fortuitous suffering without an understanding of reincarnation, which concerns the evolution of the spirit. Nothing happens by accident, including the birth of a child whose purpose in coming may be the "tragedy" of an early death. This is difficult to accept without understanding a complex of other factors including the purpose of relationships. *

People are also in the process of misusing and abusing the earth to the detriment of all of the creatures who live on it. Pollution of air, water, and soil, follows upon the materialism and greed practiced by those who have no reverence for God's creation. The Bomb is a prime example of the misuse of the advancements in science. To use atomic energy to attempt to destroy your fellow humans as well as all other living things, including the earth, is indicative of the end to which you have applied this knowledge.

Where this practice will lead depends entirely upon the decisions of every living soul on earth. We cannot

---

* Richard mentioned that the subject of relationships was important and broad enough to form the basis of another book. We are at work on it now.

make light of this misapprehension of God's Will. It takes just one misguided individual to bring about an atomic holocaust which would be devastating to the structure of reincarnation. Life on earth is essential to the redemptive plan for all, and if it is laid to waste through human folly, spiritual growth will be deterred protractedly, until restoration can finally come about. Even though the world has experienced periods of light and darkness throughout the ages of evolution and reincarnation, never before has the potential for such devastation been so real, so possible, and so immediate!

Do you have anything further to say about the balance of power?

There is another aspect of this that should be clarified now. Consider that the world normally teeters back and forth, but suddenly a new element is introduced, which is tossed back from one side to another, or rather, pulled like a tug of war. This element is the power inherent in scientific discoveries: not just the physical power but the moral power. Genetic engineering is an obvious example. Because the potential here for evil is so disturbing, good people are inclined to shrink away from the subject, preferring that it be shoved into a closet. But that is not the answer. When science opens the door, the potential for good must be examined, as the potential for evil most assuredly is. There is a potential for good in every revelation of the true nature of the working out of God's laws. The first step is to dare to imagine the good that can result. In this way the true nature of things becomes apparent. For instance, the more that you send up spacecraft, manned or unmanned, without ever daring to imagine and explore the true nature of space, the more such activities will serve only negative purposes, such as war.

What do you mean by "the true nature of space"?

We are referring to the dual nature of space including both the obstructed (the incarnate world) and the unobstructed (the discarnate world). Both aspects occupy the same space. Space research as it is practiced today is a limited proposition. The imagination is the first frontier in any exploration. Without it you are not likely to learn that we all occupy the same space, and, since you do not know that, you cannot involve yourself with what occurs in it. If you could imagine and learn to believe that there are living souls with you, around you, among you, although you cannot see them because of the differences in frequency, you would be less likely to spend millions on hardware and more likely to try to develop some way of communicating with those who are unseen by you. Fortunately, more and more people are attempting serious communication, and in time this will affect the balance of power. In fact, this will be by far the most important frontier in maintaining the balance of power and even shifting it toward construction. Those whose purpose is to work with scientific discoveries must utilize and welcome constructive discarnate intelligence.

Doesn't this offer deterrants a great deal to take advantage of?

No deterrant can affect those whose intention is constructive. A pure intention is free of the ramifications of deterrence, and therefore cannot be taken advantage of. Our great hope is that we in the unseen world can establish communications on a wider scale and guide those of you in the seen world whose purpose is constructive. If we can do this, we will without doubt be able to restore balance. It is the responsibility of those entrusted with brilliant minds to consider the moral consequences of their work.

The dangers we see all around us — drug addiction, terrorism, crime of all kinds — don't seem to have much to do with this.

They do, though, if you will stop and consider. Communication in the incarnate world, through scientific means, has shrunk the world, so that negation spreads like lightning. It should be the concern of those gifted with leadership to understand, not only that these new methods of communication can be used for constructive purposes, but that they themselves must learn how to use them constructively. Also, by opening their minds to communication between the worlds in order to learn how to cope with crime and all forms of deterrence, they are widening the possibilities in communication for world benefit.

Just how would they do that?

By opening their hearts to truth and recognizing the discarnate wisdom available to them; by asking salient questions and acting upon the answers constructively.

What will the outcome of our present behavior be?

In the Place of Preparation and in the Higher Realms, we see and know that the only possible conclusion of God's plan for all is the working out of God's Will through God's Love. The deterrants in the discarnate world see that man has become more and more influenced by their persuasion, and as a result, the success of the struggle of the Will of Self versus the Will of God is now coming down on the side of self-will. This, in turn, is augmented by the Law of Parallels. In this way, deterrants see God's laws working for them and they rejoice in the surge of Deterrent Force that results.

Each of you is responsible for yourself and your own development, and all must see the struggle that lies ahead. No one will escape the need to face up to the responsibility. There will never be a time when we can relax our efforts to regain spiritual balance. Seeing the good in all events and reacting as constructively as possible to the circumstances of our lives is essential. With the privilege comes the responsibility.

The balance in you is inseparable from the universal balance.

Earlier you suggested that simply trying to maintain the balance is all we can accomplish in life.

Maintaining the balance is the most we can expect from all life on earth, but not necessarily from each life. It takes great advancement on the part of some to overcome the failure of others. However, you are not to think that merely maintaining the balance is negative. It is the balance that creates the conditions on earth that provide the opportunity for individual growth. When this is no longer necessary, there will be no life on earth as we know it.

How could we have allowed ourselves to get into this kind of mess?

This cannot be answered in a single conversation. In order to respond to your concern in a way you will understand fully, it is necessary to start from the beginning to see just how the granting of free will brought about present conditions.

The Origin of Deterrent Force

What exactly is free will?

Free will is the right of the individual to make selfish decisions or decisions that promote harmony and construction, to choose wrong or to choose right, to choose self-will or God's Will. Self-will generates Deterrent Force, the collective energy of all thought, action or emotion that deters an individual's spiritual progress. Aligning ourselves with God's Will generates Constructive Force, the collective energy of all thought, action, and emotion that contributes to an individual's spiritual progress.

Why was free will granted?

It was God's conception of giving Himself to create individual entities of life, which brought about the existence of free will. He wanted to share the ecstasies of Godhood so all could, by their own choice, ultimately become godlike themselves — perfectly individual as well as perfectly united with Him. With the granting of free will came the knowledge of good (God's Will) and evil (self-will)—the potential and the problems that led to human development. As long as we choose evil, evil will exist.

Are you saying that evil did not exist before?

In potential only. The potential for deterrence existed, but the potential for the growth of construction also existed. Free will was the opportunity and simultaneously the temptation — it was the opportunity to learn through trial and error (cause and effect) and the temptation to be attracted to error. The vulnerability, the great adventure, is the foundation on which this subject is considered.

Has the adventure been worth the risk?
What do you think? Would you take away the choice?

I'm not sure.
Would you want it taken from you?

No, I don't suppose I would. Were there those who chose not to accept free will?
The free will of which we are speaking became a function of incarnate life intended to help us develop through choosing obedience to God of our own free will. Those who remain in the discarnate world to serve God can also make choices, but they are never contrary to the Will of God. The concept of guardian angels is an intuitive understanding of the existence of those who choose to remain perfect in their own right, serving God, and contributing to His plan of redemption for all.

But others wanted the opportunity to choose something else, to be free to make their own decisions. This gave importance to the sense of self. And so pride was born out of the determination to go one's own way, the self-willed way, the way of personal gratification.

With the freedom to choose construction, why would we want to choose deterrence as a way of life?
The fascination of deterrence (and its ultimate result, evil) is an element of being human. You speak of human faults as natural, but you must also accept that, although human faults are the result of human nature, the elimination of human faults is your responsibility. By coping with the peril of adventure, you are enabled to grow spiritually. The more you succeed, the more you

eliminate the negative karma you have built up through giving in to temptation. By coping with your adventures in the world of good and evil you are, in fact, coping with yourselves and your own problems. Even though you are drawn to deterrence and evil, very few of you are wholly deterrent. However, none is wholly constructive or you wouldn't be where you are.

Would you really classify life on earth as an adventure?

Life is always an adventure. Whatever we do, wherever we go, however we react to the circumstances of our lives, we are exploring new territory with each experience, and the adventure becomes either good for us or bad for us, depending on us.

Speaking of life as an adventure makes it seem good, but we are concerned with deterrence and evil. Why?

The reason we're spending our time on the subject of deterrence is that deterrence keeps us from growing spiritually. If there were no deterrence, you would not be in the reincarnational cycle at all, and we wouldn't be having this discussion.

Is there no attraction to good? Are we only drawn to deterrence?

The attraction of good relates each of us to the purpose of our incarnation and to our final goal. However, this is often obscured by negative force both from within and without.

What brought about our vulnerability, our apparent propensity for the wrong choice?

In accepting free will, the order of life changed. God's Will was no longer paramount, except by choice. Temptation was suddenly present — the temptation to obey our own individual desires. Being vulnerable to the fascination of this great adventure into the world of choice, it now became necessary to recognize and deal with the deterrence that we were creating.

How has the sense of individuality with which we started our adventure affected our behavior?

Individuals are born into a world of individuals, each of them part of the whole. However, they are not conscious of their individuality at first. Later, as they develop, they become aware of needs and desires that demand satisfaction. They have been granted free will so they can make choices that reflect either their own (self) will or God's Will. They tend to translate this into what they want as opposed to what they should do, which of course is really deterrence versus construction. By aligning themselves with the Will of God they too become constructive. Nevertheless, it is very simple to resort to self-will. It is a lift to the ego to think of yourself as a superior individual competing with other individuals in the real world! To seek to be just a cog in the wheel of God's construction by doing what they should do has little fascination for the self-willed.

So, now that we have chosen self-will, what then?

The decision to choose self-will is not made in a clear-cut manner. We tend to fall into a pattern of self-will through a misconception of what individuality entails. A sense of individuality is with us from the beginning of reasoning, since it is truly the perfection of our individuality, which is God's ultimate goal for us. The misconception of what it entails may creep up on us gradually with the thought that whatever we, as individuals, want to do is an expression of our individuality. Pride and vanity get mixed into this, leading us to believe that superiority and elitism are elements of individuality. Here the seeds of self-will are sown under the guise of individual expression. In using self-will to enhance and express our individuality, we may not only call on pride and vanity, but also envy, anger, and hatred—any of the karmic elements we carry with us from incarnation to incarnation, those deterrants we hope in occasional lucid moments to eliminate.

The role of pride is of paramount importance here, because it is through pride that self-will is fed. As we indulge in pride, self-will grows through its demands. Pride is never satisfied, so a self-willed person can end up ruled by pride. In trying to meet its needs, we continue to develop more devastating forms of self-will, until we become victimized by our own pride and a party to evil, at which point the forces of darkness assume power and control our destiny.

I assume that self-will begins in more subtle ways?
The practice of self-will develops self-centeredness, self-consciousness, self-aggrandizement. We become certain from early on that our individuality, our unique abilities, are what help us to achieve. But even though this indeed is true (because God so wills it) we often don't see the real truth behind it, because we perceive no further than our own selfish desires and equate uniqueness with self-will. In this way, we continue to add to our karmic problems.

Wealth, position, and success in the social and financial worlds are too often our goal. With this attitude of mind, we become willing to justify any means for achieving the desired result. We live in our own smug aura of self-congratulation and reap the rewards for which we hunger, mindless of the karmic retribution we are actually accumulating as the result of deterrence, and its active force that leads to evil, Deterrent Force.

What are the difficulties of choosing God's Will instead of self-will?

The most important element in this choice stems from our hearts' desires. In order to choose in favor of construction, we must truly know ourselves, what we really want and what our conscience tells us. This takes inner probing and a strong desire to get at the truth. Those who come well prepared are most apt to accept God's Will as their own. Because of our proclivities, it takes a great many lifetimes and much struggle to learn to choose God's Will over self-will.

I wonder why?

You don't really. You know why every moment of your life. Self-will is deceptive. It appears to be undemanding. It requires the least effort and grants the most gratification until it has usurped free will and gained control. It's very easy to slip into deterrence, or to be compulsively thrust into it, but it takes will and effort to achieve construction. Because deterrence cannot live with construction, it manages to deter it by trying to destroy it.

You say we know, but I think it's hard to tell. Wanting our own way seems perfectly right and natural.

It is never hard to tell, if you listen to your conscience and your heart feelings and live in accordance with your spiritual equipment (love, sense of truth, and intuition). In this way you see that consideration of others develops harmony. Knowing the difference isn't the problem. The problem is that self-will usurps free will.

You seem to identify self-will as negative, but isn't it through the Will of Self that we choose God's Will?

Not really. That is more accurately God's Will expressed through free will by sacrificing self-will — an act of self-sacrifice.

What exactly do you mean by self-sacrifice?

It is only through willingness to sacrifice or give up self-will, in order to become part of and fulfill God's Will, that we can render Deterrent Force powerless. Sacrifice of self-will may be called self-sacrifice because we become totally selfless in the process. Deterrent Force may appear to triumph over such souls, but only temporarily, because through the act of self-sacrifice, God's Will becomes manifest. Deterrence has thereby contributed to its own downfall. The power released through martyrdom and other acts of selfless service arouses an overwhelming tide of love and goodness, against which Deterrent Force is powerless.

It seems to me it is the fear of the loss of individuality that keeps us from relinquishing self-will.

Individuality and self-will are not truly related — it just appears so to the self-willed. Individuality is a gift given to all. It relates to our final goal and it is ours to develop. But the notion that this is done by becoming more willful is nonsense, as you can see if you think of a willful child. Such a child loses individuality and becomes like any other willful child. What is individual, unique, and particular to a person flowers with the ability to develop toward a final goal in accordance with God's Will.

The Meaning of Self

It seems to me we need a clear, uniform way of referring to self.

The self that is born comes with the knowledge of God's Will through conscience and spiritual equipment. It also comes with a sense of its own individuality, our "sense of self." As we live out our lives, that self tends to relate either to God's Will, its own will, or both. Language expresses these extremes as selfishness and selflessness.

But if selflessness is good and selfishness is bad, doesn't it follow that "self" is bad?

No. You, yourself, are who you are. You are a part of God, but you are not God. You are free to develop in accordance with God's Will, or in accordance with your own. The act of choosing God's Will makes God paramount in your life and is, therefore, constructive.

I guess people understand this by calling it the Devil's will and God's Will. The self is generally somewhere in between.

The problem with that is that when it is God's Will, it is His Will functioning through us—i.e., ourselves. Anything else that the self could choose is necessarily deterrent because it is not the Will of God. On the other hand, those who choose to do God's Will have the opportunity to construct the development of their own individuality, since God's Will for each of us is as individual as our fingerprints. When you view life in this way, and realize that the possibilities of that development are beyond your present comprehension, you begin to see the choice that free will gives you in its proper perspective.

The confusion seems to me to be that if I will to do God's Will, that is also self-will, because it is I myself who wills to do God's Will.

On the contrary, if you, yourself, choose God's Will, that may well be the opposite of self-will. "Not my will, but thy will be done" is the definitive expression of this reality. Our intuitive understanding of this is recognized in our everyday speech. We are:

Selfish	Selfless
Self-indulgent	Self-sacrificing
Self-satisfied	Self-composed
Self-destructive	Self-controlled
Self-righteous	Self-effacing

In each of the conditions in the column on the right, which are generally accepted as good, the self is limited and understands its proper place in the scheme of things. To express this in more positive terms, you say you are "self-confident," "self-reliant," or "self-contained." You are comfortable with yourself because you know intuitively that you can rely on yourself not to indulge in self-will.

Please explain the meaning of "self-possessed." Who is it who possesses the self?

All of this will become clearer to you if you think of "self" as the incarnate self, and the one who does the possessing as the eternal self.

That puts a different light on the subject. If the self is also the higher or eternal self, what does that do to the concept of "self-will" as you have developed it here?

"Self-will" refers only to the will of the incarnate self. Those in the Place of Self-Deception or the Lower Regions have adopted the attributes of their incarnate selves. They have become victimized by deterrence and evil and have taken them to themselves. That is the problem. The objective to be realized, before they can progress, is to recognize the problem and free their eternal selves.

Remember, those who are self-possessed possess themselves. They are not possessed by self. They are God-centered, not self-centered. The greater the degree of self-possession, the greater the degree of freedom with which the person can live. We admire this intuitively, understanding that it is the fundamental quality we are all seeking.

What can self-possession mean to us?

Self-possession is the goal for us all. To possess one's true self fully is to realize completely our uniqueness, devoid of all blemish, perfectly at one with God. The truly self-possessed person is the answer to God's dream of perfection for all. The intrinsic quality of the uniqueness of each one of us shines forth in the reflection of the Light, fulfilling our destiny as unique elements of the ever-evolving, ever-expanding oneness of God.

Aren't we all one in the eyes of God?

God sees us as we are — past, present, and future — our individuality and the potential inherent in it. We are all equal in our potential for realizing our individuality. We are not equal in the realization of that potential.

Since there are no two individuals exactly alike, does that not imply inequality of individuality?

It implies uniqueness. We are different, one from another, but we are all alike in our potential to reach our final goal. Your ultimate goal is an objective for you to fulfill, no one else. Indeed, no one else can possibly fulfill your goal. Also, you must bear in mind that each time you incarnate, you accept different capabilities and capacities and different conditions of life than ever before for reasons of your development. You also have different qualities from anyone else on earth. The one element which you share equally with all is the Love of God. God loves us all, in spite of what we say or how we act.

Could there be equality in our degree of self-possession?

No.

I'd like you to explain.

To fulfill self-possession to the ultimate degree, each of us proceeds according to our capacity to grow, no two being at the same level at the same time. Also, our final state, the perfect state of self-possession, is unique, not like anyone else's. With ultimate perfection comes perfect individuality and uniqueness. Equality is of no consequence.

I don't know where I am in my development.

There is no need to worry about where you are in your development. You are where you are, but what do you think about this? Are you in control? Do you possess yourself or are you possessed by self?

*How do we judge when we are no longer in possession
of ourselves?*

When you are self-possessed, you see yourself in the
proper perspective. You know who you are, truly are,
and where you want to go: where, in fact, you must go.
You recognize your relationship with God, and as a
result are humble. You know you're related to all living
creatures and that we all share and serve God's love and
God's Will.

This sounds like a very advanced soul.

You are correct. Self-possessed people are advanced
souls. However, they are just as subject to the temptation of deterrence as anyone else and must be just as
vigilant in their efforts to ward off the thrust of Deterrent Force.

In the Place of Preparation we are reminded over and
over again of the necessary elements of self-possession,
the God-centered state. With this in mind, we work to
develop the essence of one or more qualities that, when
lived out on earth, will move us closer to becoming
self-possessed.

*If there is no equality, why do we so often want to
be like our peers, one of the crowd?*

Insecurity brings on the desire to imitate our peers and
be one of the crowd, lacking faith in our own uniqueness. We are fearful of criticism and derision and resist
anything that makes us stand out as different.

Pride, on the other hand, causes us to want to be
better than our peers (we must at least appear to be
better), to stand out and be regarded as superior in our
efforts to succeed.

In neither case do we possess self. We are possessed
by self. We don't understand who we are and our true
relationship to God.

Self-possession is what we aspire to. Karmic weaknesses are what we have. These karmic weaknesses are our own deterrence, that which we have imposed upon ourselves. We reincarnate to try to overcome them. Preparation is the key to success or failure.

Then we must often come back ill-prepared?

That is true. Our karmic weaknesses may figure in the decision to reincarnate, often causing us to return to earth ill-prepared. If so, we cannot resist the temptation that appeals to us through our weaknesses. We find ourselves preoccupied with our own desires and compulsions to the detriment of our aspirations toward self-possession. Instead of realizing self-possession, we become possessed by self, our karmic self, adhering to self-will instead of God's Will.

How does Deterrent Force affect our karmic weaknesses?

The ways are varied, but they all strike at the heart of our dilemma. For instance, deterrants may use Deterrent Force to seduce people into open rebellion against restraint by indulging in compulsive activity, throwing caution and reason to the winds. If the exultant mood of self-indulgence, after having been spent, is met with regret and shame, deterrants can use even these emotions to plant the feeling that such people are victimized by compulsions and the inability to withstand them. Even though they think they will resist with greater intention next time, they often find the mind unable to cope with their karma and fall back into the well-known pattern of behavior.

Such karmic problems are never completely overcome until we reach the Realms, which signifies an end to our self-concern, our karmic dilemma. We have earned the Kingdom of Heaven.

Even though our karma becomes less and less as we absorb it through love, it can take just one moment of weakness to cause deterrants to take possession with all of the power of Deterrent Force, which heretofore has been contained. This is a devastating experience.

Can one person's experience affect others in like manner?
Yes, it can. The outcome of the struggle of each of us to become self-possessed affects all of us. Each of us is responsible for our own development, but none of us will be able to experience God's dream of unity until all of us have earned the right. The welfare of those within our sphere of influence is as important to us as our own.

Are you really saying that no one achieves union with God until all can?
Yes.

Why is this?
If you think in terms of evolution, you will see that evolution is, by its nature, particular, separate, individual. Those on the forefront of spiritual evolution presumably reach this goal first. They have become in some way one with God. However, the completely evolved state is not a reality until it is a reality for all — a whole. It is easy enough for those souls who are anxious to move forward as rapidly as possible, to overlook the power of the adversary and think that they are prepared to do battle when they may not be. To reincarnate is their overpowering desire, and if, even after much advice to the contrary, they still want to proceed, they are granted permission to do so. We are all responsible for our own development and must stand or fall by our choices alone.

Is lack of preparation a common practice?

More than you think.

There are more and more people in the world who truly don't know themselves or the aspirations of their hearts, where God dwells. Their spiritual equipment (love, sense of truth, and intuition) remains unused, rusting in the eddies of deterrence.

Those who want to win the battle with deterrence must come fully prepared to do so. If, however, their intention is to overcome karmic problems and the intention is strong even though the preparation may be weak, the strength of the intention allows the Law of Parallels to function on the side of construction, enabling them to utilize their spiritual equipment and achieve a modicum of their purpose in spite of the pressures of deterrence. They are thus able to overcome the lack of preparation to some degree.

Deterrent karma keeps us from achieving self-possession. Through these karmic elements, which we have acquired in previous incarnations, we have direct access to Deterrent Force, and through its use, the Law of Parallels augments karmic faults, thereby diminishing constructive resolve.

Aside from pride, which you've said is our greatest fault, what karmic element is the most potent?

Fear, which is an element of pride.

Whether it be fear of events to come, fear of the unknown, fear of failure, fear of success, fear of others, or fear of our own reactions to events, fear opens the door and becomes the catalyst for the admission of Deterrent Force. Fear itself is basically deterrent. When expressed, it draws to itself additional deterrence, through the Law of Parallels, rendering us unable to see clearly and unwilling to try, made captive by our karma. Thus, deterrence has free rein to bring us over to the Will of

Self, because we are unable to recognize the Will of God.

In spite of the fact that it would seem simple to achieve self-possession, since we are supposed to come prepared for the life we are to live, we must reckon with the power of deterrants to tempt us from our objective. Temptation is already concentrated on our karmic weaknesses, and so, either little by little or with one stroke (if our weaknesses permit), we may find deterrence robbing us of our self-possession. Even the first almost unnoticed step in this direction could begin to shift the balance of power until, without ever intending it, we have given up possession of our true selves — almost, but not quite.

What do you mean by that?

Through the Grace of God it is always possible to repossess ourselves. Grace provides the ever-present opportunity for the reestablishment of God's Will in our hearts.

Then why does it take so many lifetimes of effort to understand and choose God's Will?

Keep this in mind:

Reincarnation provides the means through which free will can save itself from self-will. Free will, the very thing that brought about self-will, must, through reincarnation, be the same means by which self-will is overcome. The element of individual responsibility is essential to this discussion and the key to understanding: that is, to understand our purpose in reincarnating. The plan of life is constructive. It is possible and it is provided for, but it takes time. Time is as necessary for spiritual evolution as it is for physical evolution. And like physical evolution, progress is uneven. There are many false starts and unexpected obstacles, but there is an energy of intention propelling it all, and one day it becomes apparent that progress has been made.

Deterrence

I understand that deterrence is our overriding problem. How does it function?

Deterrence is the negative element in any thought, feeling or action. It usurps Free Will by tempting it to become self-will. Once the self surrenders, it is no longer free. Deterrence has gained control.

But what is deterrence?

Deterrence is the natural outcome of the practice of self-will, which is the inevitable result of Free Will. When human beings turned Free Will into self-will, life became I before we, self-importance before universal importance, self-love before God's Love. Self before all else was the goal. With the ability to choose God's Will or self-will, there developed an overwhelming need to satisfy the ego by choosing according to the needs of the self.

Thinking about deterrence, you can find yourself drawn to the possibilities resulting from the magnitude of the problem and how it can affect everyone. As devastating as that prospect may be, it is far less important to the total scheme of things than the day-to-day reactions of each of you to the circumstances and events of your own life. How you act from day to day builds your spirit in one direction or another, and how you react to circumstances is crucial to your development.

If self-will is the inevitable result of Free Will, how did this imperfection of God's creation come about? Did God deliberately desire this deterrent possibility in His creation?

You may find it difficult to accept that God would deliberately choose to create the seeds of discontent and self-delusion in the character of His children, but the important element that overrode all others in this decision was the opportunity that Free Will offers to those who wish to reach a spiritual state that wouldn't be possible otherwise. God did not deliberately create imperfection in His children. He created the opportunity to choose right from wrong. In order to deem right the important element in their spiritual growth, they have to be able to make that choice. This implies there is an opposite choice to be made. The opposite of right (whatever their conscience tells them) is wrong (their selfish desires). Inevitably, they are tempted to indulge in their own selfish desires and try what would be wrong if they listened to their conscience. Under compulsion they turn their backs on their conscience so that their selfish desires remain their only choice.

Wrong has a fascination just because it is recognized as wrong. In this way the cycle of choosing right or wrong is begun, building up a score on both sides, often weighted more heavily on the side of wrong. Willfulness plays a strong role in decision making. So does curiosity. The need to know what's on the other side of the fence often contributes to deterrence.

Why should deterrence be so much more interesting than construction?

It's not essentially more interesting, although the struggle with it is always interesting. No one would be interested in a story or a play that was about unopposed evil.

But doesn't "temptation" imply that there is something inherently attractive about evil?

If this were not so, there would be no struggle; and if there were no struggle there would be no reason for incarnate life. The need to choose to struggle is essential to the realization of our ultimate goal. This is not a matter of God creating imperfect circumstances. It is a matter of creating the circumstances that allow us to grow through our struggle with the attractions of deterrence and the compulsions that result from our failure to recognize and resist the temptation.

It seems to me that you've described deterrence without explaining the difficulty of recognizing it and the subtleties involved. There are evils in which temptation has no part, such as disease or natural disaster, and yet they seem just as devastating.

You are confusing misfortune with deterrence. Misfortune is or is not deterrent in accordance with our response to it. However, a misfortune caused by self-will usually evokes a deterrent reaction. In contrast, a misfortune caused by God's Will usually evokes a constructive reaction.

If, for instance, a house is destroyed by a hurricane, people seldom feel defeated for very long. They pull themselves together, think of rebuilding, band together in a spirit of cooperation and love with neighbors in a common cause. If, on the other hand, a house is destroyed by malicious and purposeful vandalism, one is likely to give in to deterrent feelings of fear, anger, and revenge.

You've made the difference very clear.

It is well to recognize the difference between these two, so we can respond appropriately. If, in the former case, we recognize that God works in mysterious ways, there will surely be a constructive outcome. In the latter case we should try to understand what in ourselves attracted deterrence and what is to be learned from the experience. If we can do this, Constructive Force will begin to do its redemptive work. The alchemy of good and evil allows evil to be absorbed and transformed into good through the power of love. Natural disasters, sickness, and catastrophic conditions are given both as opportunities to overcome karmic problems and for growth and creativity. When you observe these things superficially, you see pain and suffering and sometimes death and you tend to label it all bad. But there may be another dimension, an energy at work that you do not see. Whether it is physical determination, the emergence of courage, and aroused prayer life, or a falling away of superficial concerns, there is a constructive spiritual dynamic which can result from such events.

I can understand that, but I don't think it would be much help to me if I were a starving child in Africa.

If you were that child you would be there for a reason — your choice of parents. In choosing those parents you accepted the accompanying circumstances of life, whatever they might be.

If people feel my suffering is the result of my own choice, won't that make them more hard-hearted?

It may, but is should do the opposite. If they understand that the choice of parents for some entails extremely difficult circumstances (as it may also for them another time around even though this time they are more fortunate) they should want to help. If they do not they are failing to share something more precious than food — they are denying themselves the opportunity to share God's Love.

An inevitable death by starvation in childhood doesn't seem to fit into an orderly plan for reincarnation.
There is something important I want to say to you about this. No one suffers fortuitously. There is always a reason, even if it is only to understand the true nature of suffering. Nor is one required to bear unprovoked suffering alone. God bears the hunger with the starving child. This mystical bonding then becomes a strength which will always be his. Wherever and whenever the "massacre of the innocents" occurs, there will also be an infusion of Grace.

Can deterrence contain love?
This may seem surprising to you, but the answer is yes. Those thoughts that appear to be negative, worrisome, or fearful may be brought about by concern for the welfare of another person. While such concern is motivated by love, the one expressing it is not reacting constructively and is therefore creating deterrence in spite of the concern. Because love is present, there is no evil consequence to such thoughts. However, deterrence has been added to the power of Deterrent Force because of it, even though it is of a low degree.

You must never allow yourself to become affected negatively by the problems of others. Your task, no matter how difficult it may seem to be, is to search for the solutions that lie within the problems, in order to be of help. These problems should be treated objectively and constructively. By becoming entangled emotionally in the problems of others, you do yourself no service and certainly not those who are in trouble.

That seems heartless! How can we not be concerned about our loved ones who are ill?
You think that objectivity and negativity are the same thing. They are not. It is because we are concerned

about the welfare of our loved ones that we must make every effort to consider the problems objectively, in spite of our feeiings, in order to be of the most help possible. Optimism and faith in the goodness of God can do much toward healing the wounds and encouraging the patient to see things as they really are. In fact the experience of ill people is very likely quite different than appearances seem. Optimism can help them to come to terms with themselves and their problems and gain spiritually from the experience. Your task is to try to embody constructive optimism, which can only stem from objectivity.

Evil

What is evil?

Evil is that which is devoid of good. It is the end-stage of a process that begins with self-will and ends with the inability to tell right from wrong.

It is evil when there is no thought of kinship or love, when we act in separation from others, when we assume authority over or control of others, or are indifferent to those who are our responsibility. It is evil to fail to regard those within our sphere of influence with compassion. Where there is no love, evil fills the vacuum.

It is evil when no avenue is left through which the Love of God can reach the individual. This condition results from a history of ego gratification and justification, during which the ego becomes impervious to anything but its own desires, creating a wall of defenses that resists anything that threatens its supremacy.

What is the outcome of such behavior?

When people isolate themselves from others, they are unable to relate — they can only dictate. Whether this is done through monumental self-aggrandizement (dictatorship), neurotic illness, or petty tyrannies, the characteristic common to all evil people is the absence of love.

The evil person is incapable of giving or receiving love, and so must function through other means. These means are necessarily detrimental and deterrent.

Are there degrees of evil?

No. Evil is an absolute. Evil is evil.

Underlying and motivating all acts of evil is moral depravity, which is capable of expressing itself in a myriad of ways, from disarming charm and persuasive ingeniousness to wicked and fiendish possessiveness. Appearances are deceptive, and deception is essential to the acting out of the machinations of the evil mind, which is not only filled with hate and bent on destruction, but also psychologically distorted, putting its cherished aberrations in charge.

I've been wondering about the sins of omission and commission. For instance, what if we compare indifference to the plight of starving people to overtly preventing them from obtaining food? What do you say?

All people must, in one way or another, recognize their kinship to all and their responsibility for some. We feel kinship out of love, so we act kindly toward, we feel of a kind with, the object of our love. Within this frame of reference, the sins of omission and commission are all the same since, in them, there is no such recognition of kinship either to others or to God.

Just who is our responsibility?

All who are within your sphere of influence, which includes those in your immediate environment, your family, and friends. Your efforts must be to recognize your relationship and try to help whenever possible. Individuals cannot hope to solve all the ills of the world, but they can help themselves and those within their sphere of influence. There are those, however, who are responsible for ailing humanity, whose ultimate goal is leadership and who are often in a position of power and influence. How they react to the problems confronting them can create good or evil for vast numbers of people. Although the scope of such work may be beyond your sphere of influence, you can and must become part of the love that supports all constructive effort.

What is there in indifference to cause evil?

Being indifferent to one's responsibilities is deterrent, but being indifferent to the welfare of those within your sphere of influence who are your prime responsibility, is evil. It is the very act of neglect itself that is evil.

Also, indifference is important to understand because it expresses a lack of relationship, of oneness. It is cutting oneself off from being part of the whole; it means becoming indifferent to oneself, one's real self. Such people lose sight of who they are and why they're here. They can no longer relate to their goal or to those with whom their destiny is intertwined. They have negated their spiritual equipment and conscience. They can no longer tell right from wrong. They wallow in hate and truly believe they are the center of an otherwise hostile world.

You have said that both indifference and hate can cause evil, but these two emotions seem on opposite sides of the spectrum. Is this possible?

Indifference is a powerful emotion in its effect upon those who are its recipients. He who is indifferent to the well-being of those in distress who are truly his responsibility is indeed exercising extreme although passive ill-will (evil). Hate is the aggressive counterpart of indifference.

At the base of all deterrence that stems from self-will is pride. It is through pride that we develop self-will. It is pride that blinds us to our true relationship with all others and with God, and causes us to think of ourselves as superior not only to all other living creatures, but also to our peers and therefore indifferent to them. Self-will creates deterrence. Deterrence is the cause of evil. Pride is its core. There are many facets of pride: vanity, hate, anger, fear, insecurity, indifference. They all denote the absence of love, which is the essence of good.

You have said that construction is God-centered but that deterrence and evil are self-centered. If evil is centered on each self, how does it gain its power?

We must differentiate between the manifestation of evil and evil itself. On the side of construction, as you know, everything is God-centered. All construction flows from God's Love and God's Will. This is the source that flows out and empowers each individual who is receptive to it.

Evil is the opposite. It has no center. Lucifer represents not a center, not a devil, but an individual act of self-will. Self-will is by its nature individual, separate, not cohesive. Because it is not a single power, evil becomes amorphous. It is at war with itself.

Then where does its strength come from?

All that I have said does not mean that its components cannot work together, or that it has no strength. It has enormous power and strength. It functions here exactly as you see it on earth. There are evil geniuses in the Lower Regions who dominate for a while, until they in turn are dominated. The strength and power of the Lower Regions emanates from self-will; but never think of self-will as one united will. Self-will will always be at war with itself. The danger it presents to us is that we are tempted by it. It is our weakness, rather than its strength, that is the real danger.

But isn't our weakness in itself evil?

No. But it can become evil when we are attracted to and tempted by the influences of the Lower Regions. We may then become dominated by them.

I still don't think I understand — what, exactly, is evil?

Evil is self-will that is no longer connected to free will. This is the determining factor in entering the Lower Regions. Once an individual has totally abdicated Free Will to self-will, it is no longer possible to reincarnate or to function as a human being. There is only one hope: divine intervention. This is the mission of some who come from the Higher Realms.

What is the long-range implication of the fact of a dispersed world against a unified one? I would think good would have the advantage?

The difference is in difficulty. It is much more difficult, requiring self-motivation, self-discipline, and courage, to be constructive than to be deterrent. However, someday, perhaps eons away, we shall all of our own choice be one with God. Keep this in mind: Clarity of vision is not easily come by. There is a constant need for vigilance, since the ramifications of deterrence that lead to evil are both subtle and complex, and are therefore difficult to decipher. But, by striving to live (harmoniously and constructively) in accordance with the Love and Will of God, we know for a certainty that we will not be led into temptation, and we will be delivered from evil.

II. The Sense and Meaning of Life

Adam being free to choose,
chose to imagine he was free.

—W. H. Auden,
For The Time Being

Cursed is the ground for thy sake.

Genesis 3:17

The Challenge

Living in the manner you describe seems like an enormous responsibility. Is this possible for the average person?

It seems absurd to say that you can decide of your own free will to save the world, and yet that is the only way it can be saved. However, it cannot happen unless each of you accepts the challenge that evil presents.

Remember:

You are responsible for deterrence in the world.

You are responsible for evil in the world.

You will have to make restitution for the harm you have done to yourself and to others before all can be right with the world.

You are responsible for your contribution to Deterrent Force and must, through your own free will, alleviate the karmic error that has built up as a result.

This is no simple task.

How can we possibly do it?

The power of Deterrent Force is never going to be overcome until each one of you sees your own part in its development and assumes a role in its elimination. It is our concern on this side that we join forces with those of similar mind on your side. Remember: the responsibility to overcome includes the privilege to become.

To become what? What is God's ultimate goal for us?

One universe including the incarnate and the discarnate — the Kingdom of God. Although part of God, we are as yet separate from Him. To become one with Him is our inheritance, but it takes many lifetimes of effort to achieve it. If all of us assumed responsibility for our behavior, and if that behavior were motivated by construction, we could eliminate deterrence in the world today. God's Will would reign by choice and God would be present in each of us. This opportunity exists through the function of reincarnation.

It is easy to see how others *misuse* free will, but we need look no further than ourselves to recognize the source of deterrence, which is the prime element in our own problems. We impose deterrence on ourselves by our own reaction to events. Our karma is the result of our own misdeeds, not someone else's. We may suffer from the misdeeds of others, but this is not karmic; and, if we react to the suffering constructively, we can derive benefit from the experience no matter how devastating it may appear to be. Self-will—coupled with self-justification — is the source of all deterrence. These are the fundamental elements that comprise the errors that besiege the world. Let me restate the solution: all of us, choosing to work to eliminate our own karmic problems in accordance with the plan of reincarnation, striving for construction, generating love toward our neighbors, living in faith and humility, can, with such effort, overcome the devastating thrust of Deterrent Force within ourselves. If we were all to assume responsibility for our own deterrence in this way, there would be no Deterrent Force and hence no evil.

Think of that!

I realize that free will has been our choice, but it seems too big a responsibility. Are there no restrictions on it?

The only restriction is our inability to cease to be. We are destined to live forever. Even suicide merely changes a life from the incarnate state to the discarnate, leaving the person who chose to give up one phase still alive and present in the other, with the purpose of the terminated incarnation still to be resolved.

Was it possible to realize the full implications of what we bargained for when we accepted free will for eternity?

We realized that the choice we were making required faith in the goodness of God. Without that it would have been a very foolish choice, indeed, since the choice once made was irreversible.

But life seems so haphazard!

Does it really? Think about it.

Reincarnation

When people ask, "What's it all about? Why are we here?", what is the answer?

There is a plan. God has provided us with the plan of reincarnation, a chance to try again.

Through this plan we are granted the opportunity to become perfect ultimately in the eyes of God, by growing as individuals, doing His Will to the best of our ability. In order to accomplish this, we are given free will as a means of recognizing deterrence and overcoming it, first by turning our backs on it and seeking construction, and finally by absorbing it completely through the alchemy of love.

What are the requirements of this plan?

God's plan requires that we spend time in both the incarnate and the discarnate worlds. Each world contributes ingredients necessary to the final outcome. Essential qualities are acquired in essence in the discarnate world and must then be utilized in living out of a lifespan in the incarnate world. They then become permanent elements of our nature. At the end of each life (the plan of which we ourselves have predetermined), we return to the discarnate world, where we must be able to see ourselves clearly before we can proceed with our development.

How many times must we do this?

We are given as many lifetimes as we need, with a variety of relationships and circumstances, in order to learn, to grow, and to correct our mistakes. In between we have time to reevaluate, to readjust our sights, and to prepare to try again. The paradox of this plan is that although there seems to be all the time in the world, there is really no time except now. We live in the eternal now. It is the only time in which we live. Christ taught us how. He taught with unmistakable clarity how to live now. The religions of the East have also emphasized why — there are karmic consequences, both good and bad, that will be lived through as future lives become "now." It is time for the East and the West to begin to accept one another's wisdom as God chose to reveal it.

Is the presence of evil defeating this plan?

No, absolutely not!

No matter how overwhelming deterrence and evil become, the plan of reincarnation cannot be defeated in the end as long as there is a will to live. The will to live will remain intact, because the potential in each individual plan is constructive. Even when Deterrent Force seems to have conquered the will to live through depression, despair, even suicide, the potential remains. As discarnates you reincarnate to do God's work on earth, thereby transmitting deterrence into construction. The whole secret is for all of you to live the life you came to live, by listening to your heart feelings (where God dwells) and following your intuition (the mind of the God in you, your higher self), realizing that you are unique beings with individual needs and desires that must be met if you are to live according to the plan you have set for yourselves.

I realize that the will to live is universal, and yet it seems much stronger in some than in others. Why is that?

Your will to live relates to the strength of your intention when you decided to reincarnate. Those who were clear about what they wanted to accomplish, strong in their desire to overcome their karmic problems, drawn by love to specific relationships and eager to get on with the job, always have a strong will to live. This is a tremendous help.

However, simply recognizing the importance of a successful incarnation can help those who were not so strongly intentioned in coming. As a result of trying to do a good job with whatever they have, their own will to live will be strengthened.

What comprises a successful incarnation?

A successful incarnation is one that includes faith, hope, and love, living each moment fully for itself, now. All we really have is "now." Those who spend their time regretting the past and anticipating the future are forgetting to live according to plan. All experience, all events occur "now," and how we react to them determines whether or not we are utilizing "now" constructively or deterrently. The plan of each incarnation is devised by us, with assistance from our teachers and advisors, so we can ultimately realize our potential. God's plan enables us to transform ourselves from imperfect elements into perfect and uniquely individual elements of God, and thereby affect the state of the world.

Is there a key?

Yes. Imagination is the key to gaining access to the world of the spirit. To imagine it now and live so that we can achieve effective roles in accomplishing God's Will on earth next time creates a continuity of purpose between imagination and function that helps us to begin to live in both worlds at once. And, of course, all who come to do God's Will receive help in accordance with the Law of Parallels. Therefore, the effects of those who work to conquer Deterrent Force are doubled and redoubled.

How can we live the life we came prepared to live, if we don't know what that is after we get here?
We all come with spiritual equipment — love, intuition, and a sense of truth — a conscience, and our moral values. We have been given spiritual equipment and we have earned a conscience and our moral values. We also have free will. With the use of all of this equipment, we are capable of choosing right from wrong, God's Will from self-will, construction from deterrence. In choosing, we show our colors. If we are sufficiently developed spiritually, our equipment will enable us to progress from one incarnation to the next, acquiring qualities we need so that we can achieve sufficient development to proceed to the life of the Higher Realms.

Each effort succeeded in makes the subsequent effort less difficult. The initial dead-lift is by far the most arduous. From then on each subsequent struggle grows in power as it is augmented by the Law of Parallels. The tensile strength of the spirit increases as greater success is achieved, finally gaining the higher frequency that results from growth.

If you persist in your effort to do God's Will, you will indeed blend your will with God's Will and thereby become the being that God intended.

Karma

Where does karma fit into this picture?

Karma is the consequence of deeds. The circumstances of our lives (the Elements of Development) are the result of our choice of parents. But destiny — the events with which we must cope, the twists and turns of outrageous or beneficent fortune — are the consequences of karma, the legacy of former lives. Whatever qualities we are to develop have been chosen to help us cope with our karma, which, if not eliminated, will reappear in future lives. Deterrence, the outcome of self-will, both creates negative karma and deters us from dealing constructively with the manifestation of old karma.

How do karma and deterrence relate?

Karma plays a major role in the function of deterrence. Karma is what you get for what you give. What you get, if what you give is deterrent, is the manifestation of what you have given, which you are obliged to eliminate through your own efforts. You must repay your debts in one way or another. You are required to experience what you have caused others, in essence. This does not mean you will go through the exact same experience, but you will be made to suffer in like degree, so the debt can be paid. Even after the debt is paid, you have the interest, which has built up over the period of your wrongdoing. This too is your karma, the compounded debt due. Negative karma is the result of deterrence, and deterrence is caused by karma, just as construction is the result of positive karma. These are inevitably linked.

What about karma in relationships?

First you must deal with the deterrence and karma in yourselves, then with that in your relationships, and finally, if possible, with that within your sphere of influence. Of these, karma in relationships is in many ways the most complicated. You are confronted with this constantly, on many levels. In fact, the ability to cope with relationships constructively is one of the decisive factors in a successful incarnation, resulting in beneficial karma. What you give results in what you get, good or bad. Karma begets karma.

It seems as though some have much more difficult lives than others?

This is karmic and may present an unparalleled opportunity for spiritual growth. Even those with pleasant relationships may find themselves regressing unless they reach out and extend themselves beyond the norm. This too is karmic. How you are able to spar with the present karmic conditions of both yourself and others determines your future karma.

It is negative to take on someone else's karmic deterrence. You become exhausted and accomplish nothing. This is a difficult lesson to learn. However, you don't learn by being self-protective. You must not shield yourself from it. If you do that, you will never understand it. Absorb the full import of it, and then let it go, dealing with it as constructively as you can.

Could you give me an example of how karma affects a relationship?

Two people love each other. Each has karmic problems to cope with. They react both to their own problems and also to those of the loved one. One has been granted high intelligence, but he is incapable of putting it to use. He suffers from fear and insecurity and is unable to function in accordance with his attributes. He finds himself helpless under pressure. In a past life his pride and vanity caused him to dominate his mate and abuse her, so that she was unable to live her life as planned. She became completely subservient and helpless. He had succeeded in inhibiting her completely. His karma reflects his past behavior and forces him to experience the frustration and helplessness and humiliation which is his justifiable due.

His present spouse also has to try to cope with the karma she has imposed upon herself, while the two of them strive to live with each other and bring construction into their relationship. How they react to the problems which they face because of present circumstances, plus the karmic dross that adds to the complexity of the situation, is dependent upon the quality of the preparation they have already made to cope with the circumstances of this incarnation.

Relationships can be the cause of even greater difficulties in an incarnation than were anticipated beforehand, resulting in still further problems in the future. But they can also be the source of love and harmony, which goes a long way toward self recognition and understanding, leading to construction. A constructive relationship is the most beneficial aid to spiritual progress and results in beneficial karmic conditions.

Since relationships are purposeful and continuing, I should think we would understand each other better.

The motive for your understanding is deep-seated and rooted in your attraction to and love for others. You are bound by love to your children, your parents, your husbands and wives, your family and friends, and those to whom you feel a special commitment. Failure to understand this denotes a severe regression, which must some day be overcome. Recognizing this should be a strong factor in helping to make a total effort to deal constructively with the deterrence in those you love.

Is the responsibility limited to those we love?

That depends upon circumstances and capacity, but it is never less than those you love.

What about those to whom we are related, but do not love?

Love may not always be recognized. But the members of a family unit, the mother, father, children, sisters, and brothers, always have a purposeful relationship.

What about the extended family we have today?

The fundamental responsibility is to the biological family.

What about unwanted children?

If responsibility for them is ignored this time, it will have to be faced in the future. The child's responsibility to the parents is as important as the parents' to the child. Your happiness depends on the constructive energy you put into coping with the karmic deterrence in your relationships, whether it is your own, someone else's or both. Those in otherwise depressing circumstances are sometimes happier than those in fortunate circumstance, simply because they cannot escape their responsibilities to one another.

Your karmic faults, if you recognize them, allow you to see what you dislike about yourself and what must be eliminated if you are to do God's Will and grow according to plan. This you would understand only after prolonged self-probing. When you have learned the great lesson of cause and effect, you will realize that all you do results in either good or bad karma, but both are for your welfare.

Is karma our chief stumbling block?

Not necessarily. There are other obstacles besides your karma that can pull you into a state of indecision and faulty vision, and prevent you from discerning your true identity and your relationship to God. For instance, current standards of behavior are based on self before all else. The problems you build up as a result of being too concerned about what others think of you stem from ignoring your true self and settling for your surface feelings, attempting to appease and placate them to the detriment of the spirit within.

What about beneficial karma?

All that results from constructive acts is also karma, which will bring benefit in the next incarnation. If you give love and create harmony your karma will reflect this to your benefit. But there is another far rarer form of karma I would like to discuss with you now. If, in previous lives, a soul has become so developed that he is a potential candidate to become a servant of God, his resultant karma has blessed him with insight sufficient to be utilized to spread illumination in the world during his present cycle.

If, however, this becomes impossible because he has allowed himself to be victimized by a residue of deterrence in his life, a situation will inevitably result that will cause the plan to be fulfilled after all. A condition will be imposed that renders the recipient either unwilling or unable to continue the practice of the deterrence that has held up the plan. This stems from the Love of God, no matter how it may appear on the surface. The deterrent one with the potential for great good is thereby freed to proceed with the constructive effort as a servant of God, as had been planned. Beneficial karma will prove to be the ultimate result of this effort. God's Will will be done!

Is this truly an example of beneficial karma?

It is, ultimately, yes. I say "ultimately" because it comes about only because of direct intervention through the Will of God.

Such souls earn the spiritual development that is their beneficial karma, but only because of the Love of God that has brought about their release from the deterrence, which had heretofore prevented them from becoming true servants of God. The need for their attributes has been great enough to bring about divine intervention, a rare instance but an increasing one, as it makes possible the further expansion of truth throughout the world. Servants of God work in whatever capacity is required to further the Will of God.

I suppose the awakening of Paul on the road to Damascus is the most dramatic example of the elimination of negative karma by divine intervention?

When God's presence intervenes it is because He is already there. A life like Paul's doesn't just happen. The war between the Will of God and the Will of Self was dramatized in him, but because he was already so close to God he could not escape Him. Paul (Saul*) heard Jesus because he could hear Him, and he could hear Him because he was sufficiently developed spiritually to be able to do so.

---

* "Saul, Saul why persecutist thou me? It is hard for thee to kick against the pricks." Acts 9:4

The Plan of Life

I am glad to know that there is a plan of life, but most of us are unaware of it. How can we be expected to live in accordance with it?

You are much more aware of it in the practice of day to day living than you realize. You will understand this if you allow yourself to become conscious of and sensitive to your spiritual equipment — love, sense of truth, and intuition. You will find that the quality of your life will improve and that you will become more constructive in your relationships and in your work because you have brought these qualities to the forefront of your consciousness.

Can you help me do this?

Yes, certainly.

Love is the God in you. To the extent that you allow Him to live in you, and act and express Himself and grow and work and be in you, to that extent God lives on earth through you. Your sense of truth is your inner knowledge of God's Will. It tells you that there is something greater than yourself of which you are a part, and that only by functioning as a part of that greater self can you yourself be realized. This is the fundamental law on which your sense of truth is based.

All other truths are part and parcel of this, including right and wrong.

How do sense of truth and intuition differ?

Sense of truth is present in the same measure in all of us. Although intuition is more highly developed in some than in others, it may be cultivated through belief and voluntary effort.

One's sense of truth is objective. Truth is fact and we have a sense of what that fact is. It cannot be violated. We may choose not to recognize the truth, but the truth is the truth no matter what we call it, and we know this at some level of our being no matter how deeply we try to bury it.

Intuition, on the other hand, is subjective. We sense something, we realize it, we grasp a meaning, we are guided by a feeling. We just know. But, because intuition is deeply personal, we must separate ourselves from the pressures of society to attune ourselves to it. Artists, for instance, are often highly developed intuitively. They know how to play a part, what colors to choose, the right proportions for a room. The more they trust their intuition the more individual their art becomes. That is true for all of us. The more intuitively we live, the more we develop our own individuality because we are sensing what is right or wrong for us.

Our spiritual equipment is honed anew each time we return to the Place of Preparation, so that we can be guided to the Light no matter where we may find ourselves or how dark it may seem.

You also mentioned conscience. How does it function?

Over the span of our development we have acquired a conscience, which serves as an indicator of our reaction to the circumstances of our lives. It is a monitor of our moral sense. We have built it up from incarnation to incarnation, and we have earned it by our reactions, constructive or deterrent. Those who have been able to put God's Will in charge have earned, as a result, a strong clear conscience, enabling them to take the necessary steps toward self-fulfillment in the realization of their true selves. Those who have allowed self-will, that is, the will of the incarnate self, to take charge have a conscience of weakened resolve that has little value in resisting deterrence.

It seems to me most of us tend to ignore our conscience if we can, although we certainly don't like to have a bad one.

By "bad," of course, you mean you don't like the way it makes you feel. Nevertheless, you'd feel much better if you paid attention to it because it is your guide to what is right or wrong for you at each particular moment. It is not moral law or the Ten Commandments. It is variable. We recognize this when we describe someone as having a "highly developed conscience." What we really mean is that such people are in touch with their true selves; they know at any moment what is right or wrong for them.

However, what is right for one person may not be so for another. This depends upon spiritual development, the circumstances of our lives, our abilities, our relationships. They all contribute to the messages we receive from our conscience.

Does it therefore follow that the conscience of an "old soul" is more highly developed than that of a "young soul"?

Only in the sense that conscience is an evolving function. It doesn't mean that the conscience of an undeveloped soul is inferior to that of a developed soul. It is simply not as evolved; there is less experience on which to base decisions.

That doesn't seem to account for the extreme variability of conscience.

That's because some people habitually ignore it. Conscience, like anything else, can only develop if it can function. Consequently, those with low moral standards resulting from undeveloped conscience suffer little from drastic deterrent acts. On the other hand, those with highly developed moral standards find that their consciences suffer acutely from what for others would seem only a slightly deterrent act.

The bottom line for each of us, no matter how far along we are on our journey, is that whatever we do must be in accordance with God's Will for us. We can know what that is only if we are willing to listen to our conscience.

Even if we know what is right or wrong for ourselves, acting on it is not so easy.

Of course, you must come to grips with temptation, compulsion, and the pressures from Deterrent Force. If you fail to do this you will know, because you will feel guilt.

How do you perceive guilt?

In very simple terms, it is our unhappiness at not having responded constructively to our conscience.

That seems too simplistic. For instance, what of those who feel guilty for something that happened in childhood that was not their fault?

In such cases, deterrence has resulted in evil, and evil can indeed have a devastating effect on the innocent who are involved. However, self-examination, as understood in *Why You Are Who You Are*, is helpful in seeing things truly and learning how to alleviate misplaced guilt. When we understand the difference between self-will and God's Will, we have a basis on which to establish our lives, and so the errors of the past are identified and absorbed in the effort of the present.

What is the purpose of self-examination?
It helps you find out who you are and why you are where
you are.

How does it accomplish this?
By clarifying your hearts needs and desires, which are
the same needs and desires that will lead you to God's
Will for you. They are the needs and desires of the God
in you. Getting down through your compulsive deterrent needs to those desires of the heart takes persis-
tence and a strong intention. Yet, if heeded and fulfilled,
they will lead you toward a constructive incarnation
and contribute effectively to your ultimate goal.

Just what is the process?
The first step is to recognize the elements that go into
a successful incarnation. It is well to start with prayer,
to ask for guidance in searching your heart. When
asking yourself what you really want, what would fulfill
your aspirations and your innermost dreams, you must
always try to listen to the inner voice of truth, the voice
of God that invariably sets you on the right path.

You should use your imagination to explore your
dreams. If you could dream it up, what would you most
want to do? When the answer finally floods in upon
you, try to look carefully at what has been revealed and
try to be as objective as possible. Study these dreams
of this person (who is you) and note your reactions.
This will aid you in seeing yourself more clearly.

There must be more than dreaming to the process?
The next step is to free yourself completely from measuring yourself by others. You are unique. No one else in
the whole world has your purpose, your circumstances
of life including your relationships, your goals, and

your karma. No one else can know your intention in coming this time, and therefore, no one else can judge you. You alone know why you are here. Or, if you don't know, you are the only one who can discover why.

Self-examination does not mean looking for all your faults and tearing yourself to shreds. It should start with the most positive thing you can do, search your heart-feelings: What do I really want from life? What can I give to life? What kind of activity do I feel akin to? What does my heart tell me about how to live my life? Why do I feel insecure in some situations and at peace in others? What must I do to become a more understanding person? Should I follow the way I feel about something or the way I think about it? What are my heart-feelings?

Now try to remember the times in your life when you felt your heart-feelings surface. In this way you will begin to learn who you are. From these peaks, even though they may have been only aspirations and never realized, you will begin to sense your weaknesses and strengths. You will learn where Deterrent Force found you vulnerable and attacked, perhaps over and over again until it seemed to gain control over you. However, you can regain this control if your gaze remains steady and you do not revert to measuring yourself by current standards of behavior, or any standards other than your original intent in reincarnating. This is found in the desires of the heart alone. Be sure that you separate what you really want, your true heart-feelings from your compulsions, those deterrent obsessive feelings that come from your karma. This is essential, because the first target of deterrence is to obscure not only the vision of your original intention but even your desire for your original goals.

Pride is the major road-block to achieving self-understanding. It is the most difficult obstacle to a successful self-examination, because it creates a false image. Self-examination becomes unproductive, since it is not your real self which is being examined, but the self created by deterrence.

Through a basic misunderstanding of individuality, pride was born and became the single most deterrent element to our spiritual development. Because of pride we live in spiritual blindness to truth, perceiving only a false image of ourselves. We see not our true selves but someone else, an aberration of self-will, that fits our prideful concept of what we should be.

Pride has fostered the loss of the use of our spiritual equipment, allowing it to wither away through neglect. This is tantamount to the loss of contact with God. It opens the door to deterrence and the Deterrent Force that it generates. When the balance of power within an individual shifts entirely toward self-will through pride, one can see nothing but self and the world of self. This is Hell.

What we think colors our reaction to people and events. It is on the basis of our beliefs that we function, either constructively or deterrently. Since self-examination is the cornerstone of the function of reincarnation, you can understand why pride is our most serious sin.

How can we be certain that we are doing what we should?

By making certain that the proper questions are asked, so you can know the proper answers.

Our deep feelings, those desires of the heart with which we have such an intimate relationship that we are hesitant to speak about them, those feelings and desires that are so close to our hearts that contemplating them moves us with an onrush of feeling, must be brought to the surface and acknowledged. These feelings and aspirations do not drive us to frantic activity as our compulsions do, but rather remain hidden until revealed in their fullness through constructive searching of the heart. When revealed and acknowledged, real joy is generated, accompanied by a sensation of incredulity coupled with hope! Our true feelings are the exact opposite of our compulsive feelings. They let us know what is right and wrong for us. They teach us to trust our intuition and shun the logic of our minds in all spiritual and moral concerns. The mind works well in mundane affairs, but cannot be trusted in matters affecting spiritual growth.

This initial step toward self-knowledge must be fulfilled before any further efforts toward self-realization are productive.

Are there any other clues to help us understand ourselves and clarify our intention in reincarnating?
Yes, first of all we must realize that we choose the circumstances of life into which we are born when we select our parents. Those circumstances are the elements of our development, and by responding to them constructively, we are able to raise our spiritual frequency in accordance with the needs of our goal.

Our talents, if developed, tend to become the center around which we can integrate our emotions and put them to constructive use. Often one has been given talents and abilities to act as catalysts for the application of greater concentration, better work habits, and an understanding of the value of effort as a means of spiritual development.

It is through our relationships that we come to see ourselves and why we react the way we do. None of us can grow in a vacuum. Relationships are essential to the fulfillment of our personality and our ability to cope with life. God works through people, and from our relationships we are able to learn just how important and true this is.

Relationships

How do we establish our relationships?

They develop within the circumstances of our lives. The relationships we have on earth are not accidental. They are profoundly important. Through them our lives are extended. We live beyond ourselves, continuing relationships through many incarnations. Relationships do not start or cease with birth or death. They are the most compelling factor in our choice of parents. They offer us the elements of our development (the circumstances of our lives). Our development and the development of those close to us merge. We do not develop independently. Whether our relationships embrace a great many or a very few, the quality is the important factor.

The continuance of our relationships from incarnation to incarnation suggests many questions. What about time and space, for instance?

Even incarnations that occur in widely separated centuries and countries are not the result of isolated decisions, but involve relationships. The most devastating consequence of deterrence is broken relationships, which may take many incarnations to mend. However, if, in spite of that injurious negative behavior, we have been able to love and be loved, we benefit from it in our ability to see truly. If we have been wronged we must forgive. Otherwise we will carry with us the guilt of judging another. We must forgive those who have wronged us so they can be free to judge and forgive themselves.

What about the one who has wronged us?

There is always a solution to any problem in relationships. The effort that goes into healing wounds inflicted on a loved one results in consequences, emotional and spiritual, that affect both of the people involved. Each one has an obligation in the matter. The one who has caused the problem must admit to being in the wrong, profess his feelings, and ask for forgiveness. The wronged one must work to understand the good that lies within the problem, and finding it, must grant forgiveness. They must reestablish their love for each other, recognizing the need each has for the other.

Please explain more precisely the alchemy by which apparent tragedy is transformed into Constructive Force.

When you love someone and life is simple and undemanding with no difficulties to overcome, that love can be expressed in easy effortless ways. When you love someone in spite of overwhelming difficulties that must be overcome, resources of courage, faith, energy, and endurance are called upon. You feel your own strength is not sufficient and so you ask for God's help. However, this help often comes in the form of further demands, if God knows you are capable of fulfilling them. When a person answers those demands, the influx of God's Love and Power radiates beyond the usual range of human emotions and transforms all who are receptive to it, overcoming all error in the process.

Is there special significance to relationships?

Yes. Relationships are the growth factor of an incarnation. The nature of relationships is colored by the fact that all within this circle of connectedness are heading for the same ultimate goal. They must all work out their problems by trying to assimilate the needed qualities they have developed in essence in the Place of Preparation by living them out on earth. This living out can only be done through their relationships. The entire function of reincarnation is based on relationships. Their ultimate state will be inexorably linked to their relationships because it is through them that they can recognize and measure themselves, their growth, their faults, their virtues, their morality, the development of their conscience, and their capacity for love. Linking individuality with construction (God's Will) is your major task and one that can only be accomplished through your reactions to the circumstances of your life within your relationships.

What is the essential ingredient in relationships?

In all stages of relationships, from the casual encounter to the most intimate and long-term, the essential ingredient is love, that empathizing emotion, the essence of which is harmony. By striving to treat everyone within your sphere of influence with consideration, which is an expression of love, you are at the same time adding to a needed virtue and eliminating negative elements of your karma.

What is the connection between relationships and goals?

From incarnation to incarnation, your relationships offer different facets of the ongoing problems of personal spiritual development that must be solved. In order to reach your ultimate goal, you must have overcome all problems that have arisen in your various relationships over a very long period of time and through many,

many incarnations. Your potential godhood, which has existed from the beginning of your creation as an entity, has been tainted by imperfections of your own doing. Imperfections that are the most damaging to the god in you are those affecting relationships. Your true godhood can be reached only after you eliminate all of the faults you have acquired along the way; after you earn the necessary virtues to replace them; and after you settle all unresolved disharmony in your relationships. All of you, in your own way and through your own understanding, are expected to achieve harmony — the essence of love — within all of your relationships with those of similar ultimate goal. I say similar because, although the ultimate goal may be the same, the perfected individuality is unique. You are responsible for achieving this through your own efforts within your relationships with others. The elimination of all of your personal problems and the addition of all necessary qualities to achieve your goal is to travel in tandem with the elimination of your social problems — the problems stemming from your relationships.

Your personal problems stem from your social situations, and your social situations relate to your personal problems. The two are interrelated. The betterment of one has a salutory effect on the other.

III. Consequences

Consciousness is in evolution.
There is no way an individual
bit of I-Am can stop it. Each
bit has to grow sometime: it has
to keep up with the evolutional law.

— From Betty to Stewart Edward White,
The Unobstructed Universe

The Ramifications
of Deterrent Force

I'd like to know if there's a difference between self-will and the Will of Self.

The practice of self-will has created the Will of Self, as opposed to the Will of God. Those who audaciously pit their own will against the Will of God do so to their detriment.

The Will of Self is the only way one can consider the power of self-will.

The Will of Self is the aggregate of all self-will, the power of which is Deterrent Force and the ultimate end of which is evil. Whenever humanity flaunts its own power at the power of God, ultimately, God will win out, but in the meantime humanity has managed to achieve short-term gains against the Will of God.

The Will of God includes the Love of God. Together they create constructive harmony. The Will of Self is devoid of love, and therefore its outcome is inevitably evil. Lack of consideration for others is just as damaging as overt acts against others might be because they are both devoid of love.

In summation: Following self-will creates deterrence. Deterrence is magnetically drawn to the Will of Self, which, when united, becomes Deterrent Force.

Following God's Will creates construction. Construction is magnetically attracted to the Will of God. When united they become Constructive Force.

The free use of self-will has built up an accumulation of all the self-willed thoughts and actions that have ever been expressed throughout the incarnate world since the granting of Free Will. All deterrence from the incarnate world is drawn to it. This accumulation of self-will becomes the Will of Self, opposed to the Will of God. United, the Will of Self plus deterrence become Deterrent Force.

How does Deterrent Force differ from deterrence?

Deterrent Force is the accumulation of all deterrence attached to the Will of Self. It exists in the discarnate world and is utilized by all those in both worlds who have succumbed to deterrence and evil. Thoughts are things, and Deterrent Force is the negative energy of all thought, action, or emotion that is attached to the Will of Self and deters spiritual progress. Just as God's Will generates constructive power, so self-will generates deterrent power. Whether you contribute to Constructive Force or Deterrent Force is your responsibility.

Please explain how the energy of Deterrent Force is used.

First you must accept that all experience — thoughts, feelings, and actions — become reality as they are expressed. All that you think or do becomes fact. I know it may be hard to grasp, but it is also hard to grasp the reality of sound waves if you have never lived in a technological society. In the same way, your thoughts, feelings, and actions exist at varying frequencies. Those that are inconsequential soon sputter out. Those that are self-sacrificing and heroic emanate endlessly because of the intensity of their frequency. However, we are now talking about those that are deterrent and evil, whose frequency is lower.

Is Deterrent Force animate?

It is animate, but not in the sense of being self-directed. It invariably responds in kind and amplifies the thoughts and actions of people in both worlds. To understand the effects of Deterrent Force, think of a room where everyone is silent but hostile. You couldn't be there for very long without responding to what you sense in the room. The pressure of Deterrent Force can literally become unbearable. How you respond then may well contribute to further Deterrent Force.

You have spoken of thoughts being impinged. Who does the impinging?

In order to understand this, the reality of the basic premises of this teaching must be accepted: immortality, reincarnation, and the spiritual stages of development of those in the Discarnate World. Those who have not made progress on our side have failed to recognize themselves as they truly are, and so they cling to the conception they had of themselves when they were on earth. They remain absorbed in incarnate life and attempt to go on living it, wielding power in any way they can. Deterrent Force is the means through which they can do this. Just as you could pick up the emotional vibes in that hostile room, deterrent discarnates can feel your contribution to Deterrent Force and return it to you by impinging their thoughts upon you, thereby influencing you in whatever ways you are most susceptible — through your compulsions, karmic problems, or emotional weaknesses.

Do you mean that deterrants in the discarnate world know all about me?

Only if you allow them to by making yourself vulnerable to Deterrent Force through your thoughts and actions.

What you are vulnerable to is up to you. You can be vulnerable to the Love of God no matter how difficult the situation, if you make the effort to act as required guided by your intuition. Once your weak spots have slipped from your control and become compulsions, you become so wide open to the ramifications of Deterrent Force that you can no longer gain self-control without seeking and receiving the help of God.

Are there degrees of deterrence within Deterrent Force?
Yes, there are. Once again, the Law of Parallels is involved, reflecting back the particular degree of deterrence expressed by thought and deed in the incarnate world. If you give deterrence it is returned to you magnified. Deterrence is expressed at varying levels and is magnetically attracted to a like degree within Deterrent Force and then functions as called upon. Imagine the way it works: A deterrent thought of a specific degree is automatically drawn to the same degree of deterrence present within Deterrent Force. From there it is automatically reflected back to its source, magnified in proportion to its original degree. The greater the degree of deterrence, the greater the degree of magnification. Into this automatic function deterrants intrude themselves and use it to serve their purposes.

You have said Deterrent Force cannot coexist with Constructive Force, but don't we all attract both to us through our thoughts?
Deterrent Force and Constructive Force are incompatible. Your own life is an example. You have used Deterrent Force to gain self-satisfaction and obliterate the effects of karma, and you have utilized Constructive Force to enable you to work towards God's Will for you. You yourself are neither entirely constructive nor deterrent. You have been possessed by one or the other at

different times, but never at the same time. If such an occurrence should possibly occur, you would suffer emotional collapse and mental breakdown.

If Deterrent Force and Constructive Force cannot exist in the same place at the same time, isn't it also true that as we strive to overcome our faults and add virtues — in accordance with the function of reincarnation — we have within us both deterrence and construction?

You are absolutely correct.

Then was the previous statement incorrect?
No.

Will you please clarify this for me?
You should take a moment to reflect. You need to understand the important element in this matter. All deterrence is not the same. The negative thoughts and acts that are not necessarily devoid of love, but may have led to karmic difficulties nevertheless, are on one side of this problem. Being possessed by deterrence is the other side.

What do you mean?
I mean the difference is one of degree. People can become so victimized by the effects of Deterrent Force that they're not able to utilize the strength of Constructive Force while in this condition. Once there is a desire for change, they need to pray to God to be helped to see more clearly. Then, little by little, if they are persistent, they can gain sufficient strength to turn away from deterrence altogether and allow the forces of God's Love and God's Will to heal them.

While the difference between just creating deterrence and being possessed by it is a matter of degree, humanity is never entirely free from the influence of deterrence up to the state of the Realms. All members have deterrent thoughts. However only some have been possessed by the effects of Deterrent Force. They must strive to avoid this condition at all costs.

When you say that Deterrent Force is devoid of love, you are just telling me what it doesn't have. But what does it have?

When we discuss Constructive Force and Deterrent Force, we are referring to opposites. The motivation for the function of Constructive Force is love and so the motivation for the function of Deterrent Force is hate. Love and hate are opposites. The effort to attempt to eliminate construction is motivated by hate. All those in both worlds who choose to think and act in hate or in love are automatically calling Deterrent Force or Constructive Force into action.

Because you all are influenced by one or the other at varying times in your lives, you tend to veer back and forth between the two. You are, therefore, motivated by both love and hate. In the end, depending upon the amount of intention and energy you apply, you gradually grow to emulate one emotion or the other.

Why are we so unclear about this?

It is difficult, unless you have a sense of individual purpose, to understand the real nature of this internal struggle. Although you may recognize your compulsions when they attack, you feel relief when they subside. Remorse, the ultimate reaction to compulsion, is felt less and less as the pattern is repeated. As a result, the deterrence that prompted the compulsion dominates the will, and you become a victim of Deterrent Force in all of its ramifications.

How would you describe these ramifications of Deterrent Force?

They are not difficult to recognize. To begin with, Deterrent Force, if allowed to grow through negative deterrent thoughts, can spread like a cancer, until not only individuals but whole societies are corrupted. They have opened the door to deterrants in the discarnate world who deliberately engage the power of Deterrent Force through thought to take advantage of the weaknesses and karmic problems of those involved and assume control of their destinies. Tendencies already present in members of society, such as the debasing of natural appetites, aggression, selfishness, mindless patriotism, peer pressure, or materialism, are conditions to be exploited through the particular proclivities of each, by deterrants utilizing Deterrent Force until the will, the ego, and the personality are controlled. For instance, those who are susceptible to fear because of improper preparation may be drawn into a situation where they are easily intimidated. No matter whether they give in to their fear or choose noninvolvement, the result is the same. They have become elements of deterrence through the influence of deterrants in the discarnate world.

Weakness of character due to lack of proper preparation can result in further karmic problems for many. The logical can be persuaded that reality is only what they are able to see, smell, touch, or hear; that nothing else truly exists. The vulnerable can be reinforced in their feeling that there cannot be a loving God or there wouldn't be so much grief and tragedy in the world. The creative can have their insecurities or their egos blown out of proportion. The insecure can be encouraged to repeat over and over their self-destructive responses to pressures, perhaps with alcohol, drugs, or sex. Others adopt a narrow, rigid attitude as a prop for the need to be right, when the desire to be superior becomes more important than the truth.

In all such cases people become incapable of fulfilling the intention of their incarnation, unless by extreme measures from constructive forces, they are made to see more clearly. Instead, through their deficiencies, they are adding to negative elements of their karma. The erosion of values spreads from individuals through whole societies. As an extension of this thought, I want to help you to understand that this process involves both the seen and the unseen worlds unless, somewhere, the cycle can be broken. This understanding is crucial now since scientific advances, particularly in the communications field, have sped up to a point where masses of people can easily be controlled by deterrants, who are taking advantage of these advances through the use of Deterrent Force.

I understand what you're saying, but it isn't real somehow. One is not aware of it.

You are aware subconsciously, just as you are aware of the effects of Constructive Force. But to bring Constructive Force into your consciousness and make it a part of your life, you must make an effort. You pray, you meditate, you pursue various methods of spiritual communication. Without a pure intention at the start and concentrated discipline in the act, it would be impossible for you to hold your own thoughts in abeyance and become open and receptive as you are right now. If there should be interference either from your own thoughts or thoughts imposed upon your channel of communication by discarnates (which happened in your early insecure days), you would know to stop until you brought

the situation under control through relaxation and concentration on listening.

Without self-control and attention to intention, one
can become vulnerable to unseen forces of which one
is not aware but whose purpose is destructive. However,
even if you are not aware, if you are well insulated by a
pure heart plus positive thoughts and feelings, deterrants cannot harm you. But if your own behavior is
destructive to others or to yourself, Destructive Force
directed toward you by deterrants will serve to increase
your problems.

*If you are deterrent and wish to grow deterrently,
can you call upon Deterrent Force (deterrants) to
help you?*

You can certainly call upon them, but in the long run
it will not be you they are helping, but themselves. You
will, most assuredly, become victimized.

*It's much easier to believe in answered prayer and
communication than in intelligently directed evil that
can be forced upon me from the unseen world.*

It's not forced upon you. You must consciously or un-
consciously give your consent.

*But there seems to be no retribution. Even the Church
has pretty well abandoned preaching hell fire.*

This is because it is too literal for a scientific age to
accept. However, abandoning the teaching of hell — which
is really the consequence of deterrent actions — weakens
faith in God.

That's surprising! Why?

Because it would mean that there is no sense or meaning to life.

For what purpose do the deterrants try to encourage deterrent behavior in us?

They do so for dominance and control: the struggle of good and evil. You see it in your world all the time. In Nazi Germany evil actually succeeded in gaining control, but in the end it destroyed those with whom it appeared to collaborate.

How can one become aware of Deterrent Force?

Whenever those with problems give in to their compulsions or give in to karmic weaknesses, although the initial thought impulse is their own, the rapid rush of desire that demands satisfaction comes from the Law of Parallels plus the response by deterrants employing Deterrent Force. If they then feed this force through their imagination, they will suddenly be thrust into the midst of a full-blown deterrent act that will inevitably cause harm to themselves and all others who are involved. Once the door is opened, the force of deterrence enters and takes over. Recognition of Deterrent Force in this way does not, however, alleviate its harmful effects. By the time they become aware of its presence, they have already become a party to its machinations. And they have only themselves to blame.

In this case, is Deterrent Force directed by deterrants, or does it just automatically respond?

It is directed by deterrants, with the cooperation of the Law of Parallels. Deterrent Force is always directed either by incarnates or discarnates. The Law of Parallels functions automatically.

Could deterrence result without the involvement of deterrants?

Yes, but not to any appreciable extent.

Why?

Because all acts, deterrent or constructive, result from the cooperation of both worlds. Sustained negative thoughts in your world are picked up by someone in our world and capitalized upon, encouraging greater and greater involvement in deterrence until the negative ones become captives of their own moral weaknesses.

You say our negative thoughts are picked up by deterrants. Do you mean the very first time a negative thought occurs?

No.

When do deterrants enter the picture?

Random thoughts don't attract deterrants. It is the continuing thought pattern that attracts the attention of deterrants who can take over the situation, making suggestions that bring about more and more deterrence, until the soul is unable to resist.

Is all such deterrent contact made on a conscious level?

No. There is no conscious contact or reciprocation here, as there is in constructive communication.

Isn't it possible, when one starts some form of communication, to have one's communication be picked up by a deterrent entity?

Yes and no. What happens in such cases is that the intent of the one brings on the other. If you try communication for the wrong reasons, you will contact a deterrent being. Such contact is never lucid or protected, but usually comes in short ejaculations, wild claims, violent accusations, seductive praise, or insinuation — all expressions of a deluded, deceptive mind. One's own deterrent expectations have produced the only result possible under the circumstances.

Why is the response to thought always from a person?

Because the original thought is from a person in your world, and therefore the response must be from a person in our world. We are all part of a whole within one universe, comprised of areas of darkness and areas of light, negative areas and positive areas. It is God's Will that ultimately all will be in the light.

Does our constructive thought create a similar response?

Yes, one's constructive thoughts attract and are augmented by discarnates who live by God's Will. But deterrent thoughts are joined by discarnates who live by self-will.

Are we ever truly alone?

No. You are never alone. On the constructive side you are watched over and responded to by your guardian, or in direct communication by a particular spiritual guide. Your need for privacy, however, is always respected.

On the other hand any deterrant can receive your deterrent thoughts and reflect them back, as well as seize upon your weaknesses and capitalize on them.

What about those who are just honestly trying to cope?

If you are trying to live a constructive life and find yourself thinking negatively or in any deterrent way, you become immediately aware of the downward pull such emotions foster. You must recognize this sensation as the response from deterrants, using Deterrent

Force. By your reaction, you either free yourself from this state, or you enter further into the inevitable deterrent aspects of negative thinking. To free yourself you must turn your back on the situation and concentrate precisely on anything constructive — prayer, loved ones, aspiration, inspiration — so you can once again eliminate all possible harm and return to the path of construction. Keep in mind that on earth it is not really what you see, hear, or apprehend through your physical senses that can harm you, but rather the thought behind it. It is the energy of thought alone that corrupts or frees.

When Deterrent Force is directed toward you in moments of weakness, it is directed by a person as real as any you can see or hear, and the effect upon you, if you are vulnerable to it, is just as real as an X-ray that enters your body without your ever seeing it, but that nevertheless affects you, depending upon your reaction to it.

If you do not believe life ends with the death of the body, you must therefore believe that people both good and bad continue — they must be somewhere. We call these places the Realms, the Place of Preparation, the Place of Self-Deception, and the Lower Regions, for purposes of identification. Some may say Heaven, Purgatory, and Hell. One might object that there cannot be geographical divisions, since time, space, and motion are different for us than for you. Whatever reference one chooses, they are truly states of being. They are where and what we are. They are psychological zones. We have chosen these particular references because they convey to the average person a sense of truth, and are as descriptive of the activity of each state of being as is possible now.

Judgment (Self-Judgment)

What happens after death? Who determines where we go? Are we judged?

Where you go and what happens to you are a reflection of the truth of your self-perception. The only judgment is self-judgment. It is an on-going process that begins immediately after death with your life review and continues until you are finally able to make the decision to reincarnate.

The decisions that stem from this time of self-judgment are the most influential in an entire incarnational cycle. They affect the outcome of an incarnation and can influence many that follow. It is, therefore, essential to grasp the importance attached to self-judgment.

How can we be sure of doing this?

By trying always to search your hearts and trust your intuition. A successful self-judgment in the discarnate world can only develop out of the continuing effort to know yourselves truly through self-examination, to see clearly and to react constructively to the events of your lives in the incarnate world.

To accomplish all that must be done in order to judge yourselves fairly, you are to base your beliefs (which motivate all thoughts and actions) on faith in the goodness of God and hope in the accomplishment of your efforts. Faith involves your relationship to God and hope involves God's relationship to you.

Faith: We believe in God's goodness.

Hope: We want God to approve our efforts.

Recognizing this interrelationship is the key to success in all spiritual effort.

You imply that where we are and what happens to us are the same thing. Please explain that.

Your response to the review of your immediate past life is the factor that determines where you are. If you are unable to learn from it and you feel totally justified in all of your deterrence (which has brought about an overpowering ego as a defense against the basic fear and insecurity that rule you) you are, in fact, in the Place of Self-Deception. If, on the other hand, you are able to see yourself simply and honestly, with an understanding of your failings, but still able to proceed with love, hope, and faith in the goodness of God, you are certainly in the Place of Preparation. In either case the change is precipitated by your reaction to circumstances. What happens to you is caused by what you think about it. Everything that happens is in accordance with the Law of Cause and Effect.

Does the life review differ from memory?

Yes. It is not selective. Everything is included.

Do we have to face everything?

After you die, although you are the same individual you always were, the ability to see clearly is profoundly affected by the altered circumstances.

You know that you are immortal and accountable, whether you like it or not. As a result, unless you are totally insulated by pride, your point of view about the person you see in this life review is from an altered perception, which allows you finally either to face facts, or at least to be willing to try.

Are we shown our various other past lives as well?
Not at this point. That would be too confusing. You can, however, see your immediate past life in light of your purpose for that incarnation, the choices you made about relationships and your reasons for them, the quality or qualities you came to develop, and your goal for that incarnation.

You relive not only the events of that life but your emotions — your pain and the pain you caused others, as well as the love you gave and received. By accepting it all, including the suffering, you come to see your past life more and more clearly until you are able to free yourself from any guilt you may have harbored because of your lack of understanding.

Why don't we have the advantage of that knowledge while we are still incarnate? Why is life such a guessing game?
That is fundamental to the process of life. The search for the meaning of the circumstances of your life, of your relationships, and your talents, is the means by which you grow. When you decide to reincarnate, you have accepted beginning again as a helpless baby with only your love, sense of truth, and intuition (your spiritual equipment) to guide you through childhood. Then, as an adult, it is up to you, of your own free will, to develop the faculties you have been given and utilize them in coping with your karma. Acceptance of the circumstances of your life enables you to withstand any suffering because you know intuitively that it is purposeful, both in dealing with past problems and strengthening yourself for the future. Through suffering you

can gain insight, and recognize the value of living in faith in the goodness of God.

The Life Review sounds overwhelming. How can anyone fail to benefit from it?

Some do. Those whose pride and self-will insulate them from the truth see only what they want to see. They are unable to see clearly. Since they are deceiving themselves, they are in the Place of Self-Deception, where they will remain until they are willing and able to recognize themselves as they truly are.

What if I do see clearly and judge myself guilty?

All those who so judge themselves are, in that moment, "found." They will be helped through the inevitable remorse that afflicts them, until finally they realize they have earned the Place of Preparation. This necessary development often requires protracted effort to become realized.

How can our reaction to the life review determine where we are? What if our reaction is confused and mixed-up?

That is, indeed, generally the case. Self-recognition is immediately rejected by some and just as immediately embraced by others, but it comes only gradually to most. The adjustment to life under such strange and unrecognizable circumstances comes more easily to those who were inwardly prepared for immortality. For many other souls, there is a period after arrival when nothing seems clear, nothing seems right, nothing seems hopeful. Many souls must be helped in ways that will enable them to accept these altered conditions before they can possibly be shown their life review.

Those who are confused but willing are helped to see just how and why they failed to achieve the goal of their incarnation. This experience too involves the acceptance of suffering, both their own and the suffering that they have caused others. Once they have accomplished this acceptance (which may be prolonged), they are indeed in the Place of Preparation.

On the other hand there are those who, after making some effort, find they are unwilling to accept the help they are given and cannot take responsibility for the suffering they have caused both themselves and others, but instead blame it all on others. Because of this they find themselves in the Place of Self-Deception.

You speak of help. Who is it who helps?

They are your guardians who chose to remain in the discarnate world and never incarnate. They are instrumental, as servants of God, in helping those who have chosen to strive for unlimited expanded perfection, which is possible only by following God's plan. They themselves have chosen to stay in a state of limited perfection, with unquestioning obedience to the Will of God.

How do they help?

Those who are willing to be helped are encouraged to come to terms with whatever has been revealed in their life review, particularly those for whom it is frightening and threatening. If they cannot adjust to the person they see and truly are, the personality often tends to disintegrate through fear. For these a spiritual oasis is created in which they can learn to understand the plan of their lives, what they did to thwart it, and finally to forgive themselves for what they have done, so they can find themselves in the new scheme of things. Once they are able to see themselves as God see them, they are blessed by being able to see others as they really are. Their frequency has been raised, and as a result they are now in the Place of Preparation.

The Place of Preparation

You mentioned the Place of Preparation, the Place of Self-Deception, and the Lower Regions; how do such places fit into the concept of an unobstructed universe?

These terms speak of spiritual realities, parallels of the human condition on earth. For instance, all those on earth who are evil have a spiritual affinity with one another whether or not they physically know each other. That affinity becomes a function in the discarnate world, drawing together those of essentially similar spiritual development — those of the same frequency. Here you are where you are because of what you are. In order to make this situation graphic, I am illustrating it by referring to the Place of Preparation, the Place of Self-Deception, and the Lower Regions. This is, in essence, the situation that confronts you when you come here.

What happens when we find ourselves in the Place of Preparation?

You are helped and encouraged to express your thoughts and needs as you sense them. In this way you are able to see yourself as you truly are. This is different from self-judgment, which is seeing yourself as you were in your last incarnation. Now that you are free of the guilt and the problems of your previous life, you are able to see it in the context of your development from the time you started your cycle of earth lives. You are able to review all of your previous lives, so that you can assess your development, your assets and liabilities, and particularly your needs. You also understand the joys and sorrows of your continuing relationships through those lives, what they have meant, and what they can mean.

You say we are encouraged. Does that mean we receive help at this point?

Yes, you are guided by those who, out of love, stay in the Place of Preparation to teach and assist you until you are able to make a decision to reincarnate. Also, you are assisted by some who have arrived before you, often relatives and loved ones.

You are taught as much as you can assimilate of the magnitude of God's plan, such as the need for and the opportunity of reincarnation, an understanding of God's Love, God's Will, and God's Grace as they express themselves through us and all living creatures. Finally, you are instructed about the Realms beyond by beings from the first of those Realms.

Are we still "us," or somehow different?

Intuition, character structure, heart feelings, all of the things dearest and most precious to you — your esthetics, your sense of values, and your love of relationships — are still particular to you. But you are able to see them now in the light of what you brought to the incarnation and what you did with them while you were there.

Do we have free will in the discarnate world?

God's Will permeates the Place of Preparation. Indeed, through your act of self-recognition, you have chosen to live in obedience to God in the Place of Preparation. There you are removed from temptation so that you can do this, and you are surrounded by an atmosphere that is totally constructive. In addition, the working out of cause and effect is immediately apparent, so your development becomes obvious.

Under these circumstances, how can we make mistakes?

You are still individual and function as such. It is your desire to make decisions in accordance with God's Will, but you may not yet be sufficiently developed to understand completely what that is. We often make mistakes as children do, because our development is too limited to really understand; or we may be so drawn to unfinished business or relationships that we are over eager, or we may simply misjudge our own strength and development. The choice of parents is particularly difficult, since the working out of Cause and Effect is more protracted. Your choice is the cause. The effect depends upon your reactions to events that will follow in the incarnate world. For some, the working out of a particular relationship overrides all other considerations, even though a different choice might have proved a more propitious one. In such a case, one is exercising free will in favor of the memory of a past relationship that must continue to be nurtured.

Depending upon the outcome, this choice may prove beneficial or it may prove deterrent. However, since this stage of your spiritual journey is for the purpose of making proper preparation for your next incarnation, that is exactly what you are helped to do.

Just what is proper preparation?

In the Place of Preparation, God's Love, Will, and Grace are converted into their essences — harmony, construction and opportunity. You are given the opportunity to develop under the most harmonious conditions. There is nothing to deter your evolvement.

You are offered a glimpse into the activities of the Higher Realms in order to encourage incentive to prepare well each time. This is so the reincarnational cycle can be left behind as soon as possible and you can proceed on to the life of infinitely greater purpose, love, energy, and creativity offered to you in the Higher Realms.

The higher frequency you have attained enables you to set about to prepare for your next incarnation with confidence. Because you now see more clearly, you are more aware of the problems you must overcome and the qualities to be acquired in essence, in order to live them out in the incarnate world and make them permanent elements of your eternal being. You work on a particular quality, or maybe several qualities, depending upon the importance of reincarnating sooner and accomplishing less, or waiting until later, with the hope of accomplishing more. You are guided in this choice and taught the essential values of the qualities you need. You concentrate on their realization in essence through the use of the imagination and intuition.

I'm not sure I understand exactly what you mean by quality.

Let's start with yourself and I think you'll understand exactly what I mean. Although at first you might think you would like to acquire a more attractive personality, a ready wit, a brilliant mind, on reflection you realize those things are gifts; they constitute part of your Elements of Development. The qualities that you must have are needed to build your character: honesty — not the kind that has anything to do with "little white lies," but the kind of honesty that enables you to know yourself; energy, which has nothing to do with activity, but which is so concentrated and centered on God's Love that power emerges; humility, not a false image, but the desire to simply accept God's Will without question. If you think about yourself, as you do in the Place of Preparation, you will see the importance of achieving needed qualities in sufficient quantity to build a character that withstands Deterrent Force and functions as a part of God's Love and God's Will. You must also recognize your karmic problems and work to acquire and/or to strengthen the qualities you need to overcome them. After which, if you so desire, it is time to prepare specifically for the next incarnation. This all requires concentration, the duration of which depends upon your goals. Your sojourn in the Place of Preparation could take thousands of years by your time or much less. Desire along with concentration affects the span.

The final decision is the choice of parents. This choice will control the circumstances of the incarnate life to come. These circumstances become the elements of your development, depending upon your reaction to them. The choice of parents is conditioned by your relationships and how they have evolved, your karma and what contribution it makes to the decision, and finally, your heart-feelings concerning this particular decision and the goal that has been set for this incarnation.

No one exists in a vacuum. Each person is born into a situation already affected by both constructive and deterrent forces. The balance between the preparation that one has made and the circumstances that have been chosen as the result of the choice of parents is both crucial and complex.

Who? Why? What? Where? When?

Just imagine being confronted with these possibilities in your next life! You might think that, of course, you would pick parents who would provide something wonderful. But this is not necessarily so.

Why not?

Because there are other considerations, all relating to your purpose in reincarnating. You must overcome your karmic problems, or at least some of them (you have been working on this in the Place of Preparation each time you've been there). You must be able to add quantity to the qualities you've developed in this place by living them out successfully on earth. You are to strengthen your good relations and rectify your bad ones. You need to make every effort to live a constructive life in order to progress according to plan. You must accurately gauge your strength to persevere, as well as the deterrence inherent in a particular situation, and decide just how much you can take on.

Just how is a right choice determined?

When we refer to right choice of parents, we mean the parents who will offer circumstances that will best enable a person to live out the qualities gained in essence, in order to acquire them permanently.

However, any choice of parents, even though it is not ideal, can become constructive if one reacts constructively to subsequent events. A particular quality such as courage might be better acquired under difficult, trying circumstances than pleasant, bland ones. However, fear can be felt in all circumstances if one is so prone — courage is needed in all situations to one degree or another. No choice of parents is of itself ever totally wrong or totally right, since the determination depends upon one's reactions to the circumstances and events that follow. The most one can know beforehand is the potential inherent in the choice. One's goal for this incarnation may be altered because of the choice of parents, but it can always be turned in the right direction.

Do we tend to make the choices that are right for us?
Not always. However, sometimes seemingly poor choices
are made, not necessarily because of insufficient preparation, but because of compelling reasons having to
do with particular circumstances. For this reason and
for many other reasons, both positive and negative,
parents in difficult situations are often chosen. On the
other hand, deterrent religious or moral values or de-
moralizing social conditions, which could be included
within the choice of parents, may lead either to growth
or to stultification. Similarly, favorable circumstances
may lead to either, depending upon the wisdom of the
decision to reincarnate as well as the reactions to the
circumstances and events which follow.

It is possible to choose parents out of self-will?
All that takes place in the Place of Preparation is influenced by the Will of God. However, there is always the
possibility that your opinion of what is right for you
may be colored by your attachments to specific relationships. Through these influences you sometimes choose
what may not be the best possible situation. You may
even know this, but want to make the choice anyway
because of the powerful draw the relationship has on
you. Because it may not be the best choice, it is to
some degree deterrent. This decision may cause you to
repeat past errors. To this extent, deterrence can be
present in the Place of Preparation.

Then what must our concern be?
You are to be concerned with those elements that your
choice of parents provides and how to utilize them to
achieve self-possession, or how they affect you negatively, allowing deterrence to rule your life. All circumstances of life can be turned either into constructive

elements of your development, or the means through which you lose your true identity and commit yourself to deterrence. In order to gain a measure of self-possession, you must come well prepared to cope with your karma and the circumstances of your life.

Am I ready to reincarnate now?

Not quite. Once the decision is made concerning your parents, you are allowed to review your various lives once again, to confirm how your past parent-decisions developed, and therefore, whether or not this present decision truly fits the need as you see it. If you entertain any doubt at this point, you have the opportunity to reconsider your choice, giving your heart-feelings and intuition full rein before coming to a final conclusion. Every consideration is made to provide the opportunity for the most propitious choice. The choice is yours to make. The results are yours to cope with. All the help available cannot alleviate the responsibility you have for your own decisions.

It surprises me that so many of us are so undeveloped — spiritually, intellectually, morally. With all this preparation, you would think we'd be more competent.

You must remember that the only requirement for leaving the Place of Self-Deception is to see yourself as you truly are. When you have done that your frequency is accelerated so that you are, in fact, no longer there but in the Place of Preparation. However, that does not guarantee that you will profit from the help you receive. That is up to you.

But if you have not profited, how can you be ready to reincarnate?

That may be the very reason for the incarnation. It might be beneficial to try again and fail, if only to learn that incarnate life takes more resources than you have been willing to develop. In any case, you are not in a position to and should not make judgments of this kind. You don't know another person's history, relation-ships, karmic problems, or reason for coming. The Place of Preparation is like a school. There are some who graduate, but there are others who have to leave early. And there are still others who have to be pushed and pushed in an effort to get them to overcome the fact that they are comfortable and prefer not to leave. That can be a real temptation — the eternal student. However, this is fundamentally a place of opportunity and development. The realization that growth is ahead on earth should give a sense of hope and expectancy and alleviate the fear of taking the plunge!

The Place of Self-Deception
and The Lower Regions

We have been discussing what happens to those who see themselves clearly, but what about the ones who fail or don't really want to see clearly? What are they doing and where are they?

In our first book, *Why You Are Who You Are*, we provided only a glimpse of the essentials needed to live a constructive life, because we wanted that teaching to serve as a primer. Although the Lower Regions were mentioned, the entire complex picture was not drawn at that time in order to avoid confusion. What follows concerning those who do not go on into the Place of Preparation will be spelled out, in order to impress upon you the extreme importance of individual responsibility and the circumstances which surround it.

Although we have discussed the Place of Preparation and the Lower Regions in terms of location for simplicity, they must be understood as states or conditions of being, having to do with frequency, which is the number of vibrations per unit of time. It is because of differences in frequency that our two worlds, the incarnate and the discarnate, can exist in the same space. The frequency in the discarnate world is so intensely rapid as to be transparent and undetectable by those in the incarnate world, where the frequency is very much slower. The frequencies of the discarnate world allow no obstruction whatsoever. One doesn't move around objects. One passes through them. As you know, this is not the case in the incarnate world.

What has frequency to do with the discarnate experience?

Whatever frequency the discarnates have realized is the frequency to which they are drawn. This is, of course, the frequency of the eternal being, which has been affected one way or another by the behavior of the incarnate being. In the Place of Self-Deception their attributes are apparent to all and they can recognize a fellow traveler immediately. They see themselves, and they see themselves in others. Since they are all there for the same reason, this is not difficult. They approve of what they see.

If we see ourselves as we are in the Place of Self-Deception, isn't that the requisite for going on?

You might think so, but let me present it to you this way: You see yourself as you are. That is not the same thing as seeing yourself as you truly are. It is *that* self that you must be willing to see. That takes a great deal of courage, because when you see that self clearly, you realize how far you have yet to go. When you see yourself as you are now, when you recognize yourself in others, you may rationalize and excuse, you may even like and admire. But that is no longer possible once you have seen your true self—your potential and your problems.

This situation is also true on earth. Those who are smug and self-satisfied have no idea who they really are. That is why humility is such a virtue. What humility really is, is seeing yourself truly. "Blessed are the meek, for they shall inherit the earth." They will be able to come back and have constructive incarnations. "Blessed are the pure in heart, for they shall see God." They are able to see things as they truly are. They can go on to the Realms.

So when we speak of self-recognition, we may well recognize the self we have been and the self we are, but we must also be able to recognize the self we can be. In the Place of Self-Deception, unless you can be brought to seeing yourself truly you continue to deceive yourself about who you truly are in an effort to bolster the self-will that holds your deceptive self together.

Is this Purgatory?

The concept of Purgatory as the place to purge yourself is an acceptable description of the intention of the Place of Self-Deception. This is possible only where there is no one to rule over, no one else to blame, no one. This is possible here.

I understand that we are drawn to the Place of Self-Deception because of the frequency at which our spirit vibrates, but how do we learn where this frequency belongs?

The degree to which you have achieved self-possession determines the degree of frequency you can reach in the world of spirit. How you have worked on the incarnate side to understand yourself and realize who you are contributes in large measure to your experience on the discarnate side.

What we believe has a marked influence on just where we go. For example, those whose intention has been constructive, but who need clearer vision to enable them to move forward, are permitted to go through the process that has been described above. They learn about their past lives and how well they functioned in them. By seeing all the times they inflicted harm on others, and by suffering the consequences of their deeds, they are purged of guilt and enabled to proceed with a clear conscience. As a result, they strive to overcome some negative elements of their karma. This realization raises their frequency to that of the Place of Preparation. This is the function of the Place of Self-Deception according to God's Will.

However, those who have lived relatively good lives, even "religious" lives, but have done the right things for the wrong reasons, such as believing they are among the "chosen few" destined for "Heaven," will of course get just what they imagine. Surrounded by their fellow believers to whom they are immediately attracted, they will create for themselves an atmosphere that fits their conception of "Heaven." Here they abide with the delusion that they are indeed the chosen few. This form of blindness is very difficult to overcome.

The ones whose lives have been dominated by the need for sensual satisfaction to the detriment of all else in life, the compulsive, addictive ones, find themselves in an atmosphere of extreme urgency with others like them who are attempting without success to satiate the insatiable. The memory of overpowering desire remains with them with no possibility of satisfaction — a pitiful state.

We are primarily concerned, however, about those who are ruled by self-will, since they comprise by far the greatest numbers. These are the people who feel that they are never wrong and that their wills are superior and certainly dominant. They reject the help that is offered that would enable them to move on, preferring instead to remain with their own kind, trying to prove their superiority while basking in the satisfaction of self-approval — a frustrating state.

In all of the various levels and conditions of frequency in this spiritual environment there are varying degrees of self-deception. It is indeed the Place of Self-Deception. Even though God's Grace provides the ever-present opportunity for change, we see that too many misuse and abuse this opportunity for their own purposes out of compulsive blindness to truth, clinging to self-will and spiritual isolation.

How do the self-willed behave?

There is constant deterrent behavior to themselves and to others — in this frequency and also to you in the incarnate world. They keep trying to justify themselves, and so they direct their thoughts to the ones on earth who are vulnerable. This often is manifested as inexplicable deterrence. The ones on earth become vulnerable to these efforts through their compulsiveness and karmic problems. However, this force cannot reach those of strong will who are unwilling to be seduced by deterrants.

Do the people who have not progressed to the Place of Preparation remain permanently in the situation in which they find themselves in the Place of Self-Deception?

Not necessarily. If they have even a spark of desire for change and are brought to recognize themselves as they really are, they can go on to the Place of Preparation. Having learned the hard way, they may do well in their next incarnation. However, those who make no effort, in spite of the help that is offered, remain where they are, coming more and more under the influence of those in the Lower Regions. I cannot describe this world in terms of your world; I can only say that symbolically, the longer they remain, the more they develop deterrently in cooperation with those in the Lower Regions. Conditions for them in the Place of Self-Deception become more and more dense with each deterrent act, until at last, having embraced evil, they sink into a common condition of lowered frequency. This is Hell or the Lower Regions. To ever emerge from this final condition is only possible with Divine intervention through very advanced souls who try to help. Those who are responsible for horrendous evil, on the other hand, go directly to one of the various conditions in the Lower Regions. They are already in a state of Hell.

How did these negative regions come about?

Both the Place of Self-Deception and the Lower Regions are states of being in the discarnate world that have resulted from aberrations of the mind caused by self-will in the incarnate world. Although the Lower Regions are a state of being, the frequency level there is the lowest within the discarnate world. This conditions the atmosphere in which life exists, because all who are there create the same atmosphere. Although each has an individual frequency, they are all in it together. They are all dedicated to evil and share pride, which is the common cause of their problems. In the Place of Self-Deception it's everyone for himself, but in the Lower Regions, they are united in a common cause—world domination.

Do they have any effect on the incarnate world?

They do indeed. Through Deterrent Force they may concentrate energy on self-justifying elements, such as unfinished deterrent plans that they think are destined to work out, attempting to reclaim the earth as their kingdom, and they involve those on earth who are already deterrent and vulnerable to evil. The more you learn about this, the more you will see that all people on earth tend to live in either the positive or negative kingdoms, and this choice is crucial to development. Whenever you are even brushed by deterrent negativism it could become evil, so it is important to latch onto something positive — a thought, a prayer, an action, any expression of love. In this way the influence of the Lower Regions on earth is lessened. The effort to help those in the Lower Regions can only be attempted by those who have sacrificed self-will completely. They are in a very advanced spiritual state. The best the rest of us can do is try to grow in that direction.

Is the major thrust of deterrants on the incarnate world from the Lower Regions or the Place of Self-Deception?

I would have to say the Lower Regions exert the greatest influence toward evil. Their ultimate goal is world domination by the Will of Self. This frequency houses the souls dedicated to evil. The ones who choose to stay in the Place of Self-Deception and refuse to see and acknowledge themselves as they truly are still have the opportunity to move forward. One spark of desire for change at any time will bring constructive forces to help restore them to reality and health. But the longer they stay the greater the influence from the Lower Regions becomes.

Those in the Place of Self-Deception are hoping to involve incarnates in more and more self-willed acts that lead to deterrent behavior. This effort influences incarnates toward aberration and faulty vision. This is to ensure that when they arrive in the Place of Self-Deception, they will see themselves only as they want to see themselves and will choose to stay where they are.

Those in the Lower Regions are using the weaknesses of incarnates to solidify the need for the satisfactions of evil practices. Once the incarnates' need for emotional gratification becomes apparent, they are encouraged by deterrants to act in ways that result in deterrence and evil. The more this path is followed, the greater the need for satisfaction, until nothing short of overt acts of violence will do. Evil has gained a collaborator.

Those in the Lower Regions also gain disciples from the Place of Self-Deception who are blind to truth. Because they have attached themselves to the gratifications that result in evil, it is easy to encourage them to join the dedicated ones in the Lower Regions in order to help bring about world domination by the Will of Self. When adjectives such as dark, murky, and slimey or hell fire and brimstone are used to describe the Lower Regions, the purpose is, of course, to convey an idea of the various conditions there by means of similes that are vivid and understandable to you. Just as the underworld on earth has its own fascination deriving from the use of power, so has the spiritual underworld. Remember, those who are here have lost all sense of truth, but they can still recall the past and anticipate the future.

Can they recall all past lives or is that shut off as it usually is for us incarnates?

No. Hindsight extends to former lives and foresight is clear, so that they, as well as we, can see possibilities ahead. This is true of all who are in the discarnate world, no matter where. Intent, not event, is seen, but for deterrants it too is colored by deception.

Under those circumstances I am surprised that there are those who allow themselves to go to the Lower Regions.

Spiritual blindness is also a reality. Even though the truth is available, many are unable to see it.

I gather from what you have said that some in the Lower Regions are inactive and some are active. What makes the difference?

Those in the Lower Regions who are inactive have committed horrendous crimes of evil upon others for the sole purpose of self-gratification. Their perspective is riddled with evil. As a result, in the incarnate experience crime has become a means of releasing tensions. There it is perceived as an antidote to the extreme anxiety that results from the effects of malicious wrongdoing. The climax achieved in the evil act offers a sense of emotional release. An appetite for evil is thus built up, which has to be gratified. This continuing pursuit leads to total inactivity in the Lower Regions, out of reach of Constructive Force.

There are many, however, whose thoughts and acts have resulted in evil, but who have not developed a continuing pattern that leads to complete downfall. Their efforts have taken them to the Lower Regions, where they refuse the help which is offered them. They prefer to align themselves with the Will of Self, which has regulated their lives and will continue to do so as long as they remain dedicated to evil. Although it would take extreme measures by servants of God to bring such souls out of this morass, the possibility is always more important in the eyes of God than evil intent. Therefore these souls are free to function as they wish.

Please comment on Christ's emphasis on the "everlasting fire."

The problem is in reconciling the torments of Hell as just retribution with the concept of the Lower Regions as a choice. This is reconciled when we understand that it is a continuing choice. The choice is made second by second, hour by hour, day by day, until the time comes when the choice is a fact. Choosing evil and doing it are suffering and torment. Equate this with war, which is Hell on earth, and yet people continue to choose it.

Isn't it true that we often choose war only because we are afraid of being at someone else's mercy?

For whatever reason, it is still a choice. Christ told us to "turn the other cheek" because it is only through the act of self-sacrifice that we remove ourselves (our eternal selves) from the power of Deterrent Force. The Twenty-third Psalm expresses this thought succinctly: "Yea, though I walk through the valley of the shadow of death I will fear no evil" — Evil is understood as something altogether different and worse than death.

Those who have chosen evil, who wish to be evil, who believe that their evil choices are right, who deliberately refuse to allow the good in themselves or in others to exist, who have destroyed their own conscience and spiritual equipment, so that they no longer love, sense the truth, or grasp it intuitively, those who seek to make the self all powerful, go to the Lower Regions and find themselves beyond the reach of moral law. The "fire that never shall be quenched" is the emotional torment, the fear and hostility, the anger and futility that consume them inwardly.

How do those in the Place of Self-Deception affect us here on earth?

Those on earth whose karmic problems prompt them to think and act deterrently toward others, and consequently toward themselves, are susceptible to the power of Deterrent Force as utilized by deterrants in the Place of Self-Deception. They recognize a possible convert to the cause of deterrence.

The Law of Parallels dictates that a force stemming from deterrence evokes a like-force. As long as those in the Place of Self-Deception succeed in deceiving themselves, they will use this force to the detriment of others. This is sometimes mistaken for communication, especially by those who are deterrently disturbed on earth, or when drugs have eliminated normal barriers. In these cases, what is received is confused with their own psyches.

Is the Deterrent Force from an individual in the Place of Self-Deception or the Lower Regions particularized to a specific individual, or just emitted in general toward those who are receptive?

Both individuals and groups on earth can be influenced by the concentration of the deterrants from whom the deterrence is originating. Deterrent Force is used by those in the Place of Self-Deception and the Lower Regions to augment and extend their thoughts in an effort to influence and win greater commitment to the cause of deterrence and evil. It could be that those who allow themselves to be affected by this kind of negative effort continue to be influenced adversely by associations that were deterrent, after the associates have died. A person might be inordinately preoccupied with the one who has died, because the force of the presence is felt, or he might be excessively frightened of death because negative influences are felt.

Now this does sound like some kind of thought transference. It isn't?

Not truly. When those on earth attempt communication in these cases, the messages received are distorted and one-sided. True communication cannot take place between the earth and either the Place of Self-Deception or the Lower Regions.

If there is no communication, how do the deterrants affect us here?

It is the redundant negative thought originating from the incarnates that attracts deterrants in the Place of Self-Deception and the Lower Regions. Once attracted, they utilize this deterrence, which has been augmented by the Law of Parallels to the detriment of their victims in the incarnate world. This all takes place on an unconscious level as far as the victim is concerned. The incarnates have no relationship with the discarnates here. They are led to believe that the increased pressure toward deterrence and evil that results is caused by their own thoughts.

Is it better to forget about deterrent or evil individuals after they die?

On the contrary, this is the other side of the coin. Deterrence and construction travel both ways. Prayer and positive thoughts can help all those in the Place of Self-Deception and the Lower Regions, and at the same time protect you from any negative force coming from them. It is essential that you understand the ways in which deterrence exists simultaneously in both worlds. What is seen and what is unseen are equally real, just as God's Grace is real. Those manifestations of which we are aware are manifestations of an unseen force.

I thought they were manifestations of self-will.

Self-will is the magnet that attracts Deterrent Force, so what seems an understandable wish or tendency, such as ambition or escapism, can soon become unmanageable. The magnetic attraction works in both worlds simultaneously, so that not only is the individual affected, but all those in both worlds who are concerned about his welfare. The frequency of their spirits is lowered as a result. However, if you are able to create an atmosphere of construction around the individual it can protect you and also affect him positively, raising the frequency.

You have said that deterrence, as it functions in the Place of Self-Deception and the Lower Regions, tries to claim and keep its own kingdom. I don't understand this. Is deterrence an entity in itself? How does it claim its own kingdom?

Deterrence is a force in the world. This force is the accumulation of all deterrent thought and action. This force has a will. It is the aggregate of all self-wills of individuals — the Will of Self as opposed to the Will of God. Thoughts are things, and therefore when deterrent thought is expressed, it contributes not only to deterrence but also to self-will as its motivation. Deterrent Force is ruled by the Will of Self, which in turn uses it as the means of gaining converts to the cause of deterrence. Just as the Will of God works through people, so the Will of Self works through people. Free Will was God's gift to us. Self-will was our response.

Is there a single directing intelligence that rules Deterrent Force?

You need to grasp this concept clearly. The intelligence that rules Deterrent Force is that of man. The Will of Self is the will of man alone. The Will of God is the Will of God. The nature of the one is deterrence, the other construction.

The power of the Will of Self, the collective will of all self-willed souls, is Deterrent Force, and this is used to gratify the Will of Self as expressed by man, incarnate and discarnate alike.

The Power of the Will of God, enhanced by the will of all constructive souls, is Constructive Force, and this is expressed through human actions, incarnate and discarnate alike. The Will of Self is the result of Free Will. Selflessness has become selfishness. There is, of course, no singular motivating force behind deterrence and evil, such as the concept of a Devil or Satan. This is merely man's subconscious effort to avoid responsibility for deterrence and evil in the world. The motivating force of construction is God. The motivating force of deterrence is man.

Construction is by nature harmonious, and so all who are constructive work in harmony toward a common goal — perfection. Deterrence is by nature inharmonious, and so those who are deterrent create discord with each other, each working for himself. Construction becomes a united effort. Deterrence is in continual disruption.

Richard, how then can deterrence gain such a foothold against construction?

Because it is present in all of us. All who seek the constructive path are constantly working to eliminate the deterrence that is present. Without constant diligence and vigilance, deterrence can easily regain its foothold.

Are the objectives of those in the Place of Self-Deception and those in the Lower Regions the same? You link them together, but this point is not clear to me.

The objectives of both are to bring souls to the Will of Self. Frequency denotes gradations of negativism from deterrence to evil. Those at the deterrent level have a specific frequency. At first this frequency is the same as that of those who, after learning to see themselves truly, move on to the Place of Preparation. However, once they stop trying to see themselves clearly and choose to remain where they are, they continue to practice self-deception, coming more and more under the influence of the evil ones in the Lower Regions, until they finally lower their own frequency to that of the Lower Regions and become advocates of evil.

Those in the Place of Self-Deception are not united in their efforts. Everyone is out for himself, trying to win the most converts to the Will of Self.

In the Lower Regions, however, conditions are quite different. Those who are able to function at all, function in unison under the banner of evil, in the cause of world domination. From this unified group, the evil geniuses from the Forces of Darkness whose objective it is to conquer the Forces of Light by vying with them for the souls of all on earth who are uncommitted.

The Realms

What can you tell me about the Realms?
I can only give you a glimpse at present. There is so little concerning the activity there that can be explained lucidly that we must settle for the fundamental facts that you can grasp.

How many Realms are there?
There are seven Realms, which relate to the seven purposes which must be assimilated before we can reach the ultimate goal. Each Realm has a particular purpose. All those who have reached the Realms have these purposes to assimilate, and each stage is determined by a specific degree of frequency, growing more rapid, and intense as one progresses.

The seven Realms and purposes are:

Realm I	Evolution
Realm II	Enlightenment
Realm III	Creativity
Realm IV	Wholeness
Realm V	Individuality
Realm VI	Purity
Realm VII	Unity (God's Will)

Those who reach the Realms are informed of the need for acute clarity of vision, which is required to understand the seven purposes they must assimilate before they can hope to attain their ultimate goal. They are told that from now on they are on their own. Further development is solely up to them. In Realm I they are working to assimilate the essence of evolution, and in this process they are able to help people in the Place of Preparation as an aid to grasping the essence of their purpose. However, from then on, except possibly for a necessary decision to reincarnate for the betterment of humanity, the effort becomes more singular and arduous. Here we apply what we have learned of the value of effort.

I thought you have said that those in each Higher Realm help those in Lower Realms. If this is so, how can we be entirely on our own?

You haven't considered the nature of growth in the Realms. Since those there are striving toward unique individuality in its perfected state, they alone are aware of what must be done and are capable of achieving it. In the realization of unique individuality, the individual must not only be able to see what is entailed, but must arrive at the unique result before enjoying the ecstasy of oneness with God.

The help that is received at each level includes only such elements as encouragement and love from those who have reached the next higher level. And yet, all such assistance raises the frequency of the souls at both levels, proving that everything is possible through God's Love and God's Will.

How do purposes and goals compare?

In the discarnate world the concern is chiefly with goals. Each of you has a particular goal. However, as you work toward that goal, you are also working toward one, and finally all of the seven, purposes. Every incarnation offers the opportunity to pursue one's goal, or at least to pursue an element that will lead to it. You come to an incarnation prepared to do so. The quality that you come to develop in quantity is part of that process. For instance, if your final goal is leadership, you may have acquired the quality of courage in essence, which you have come to develop in quantity. You will have chosen your parents with this in mind. In doing so you might serve any one of the purposes, just as your goal of leadership, once achieved, can ultimately be used to serve all of the purposes.

The final goal is fixed. It is part and parcel of the individuality with which you were created, but the ways in which you pursue your goal are infinitely varied and differ with each incarnation. The goal determines the quality that you reincarnate to develop in quantity. In trying to achieve your goal, you are inevitably working toward one or more of the purposes. Just because you may have finally overcome your karmic problems through love, it doesn't follow that life becomes easy from then on. In fact, it becomes much more difficult because the stakes are perfection of spirit and perfection is won only with the greatest effort, applied with the utmost concentration — on your own!

In order to reach the ecstasy of godhood by achieving your final goal, you must acquire all of the elements necessary through mastery of the seven purposes, making them your own, elements of your final goal.

The proof of your development is found in the ability to exist in the more rarefied atmosphere of the Higher Realms, which become more refined, the vibrations more rapid, as you progress from one realm to the next. Survival depends upon the degree to which you have been able to purify your own unique quality, and so speed up your frequency, which is an integral part of the ultimate state. If you find you cannot survive the atmosphere (sustain the frequency), you revert to the previous stage and continue with your efforts to develop sufficiently to move on. At this point, the will becomes an overriding influence. If you think you are ready to move on, you attempt to do so. If you obtain the higher frequency necessary, then it becomes a matter of the ability to maintain the concentration that enables you to sustain the frequency. If it is not possible, you automatically return to the next lower Realm.

Are there relationships in the Realms?

Yes, indeed. Although the growth effort is a singular process (there are no guidance advisors or teachers), those in the Realms use their relationships there to gain the understanding and development needed for clearer perceptions that lead to growth and higher frequencies.

Richard, you just said they were on their own, that it was a singular effort?

And so it is. Those in the Realms love and encourage one another, especially those who are related. However, this love is never obtrusive, but is respectful of the degree of function that has been achieved.

The Realms are the Kingdom of God. The presence of God is manifest. Those who are there have learned who they are and just what their contribution to the ever-expanding Godhead is to be, and they strive to achieve the perfection they long for. In the Realms one is bidding for the highest stakes, and so the effort required and expended at each stage of development grows and becomes more and more complex in relation to one's increased capacity.

Have we understood the nature of our ultimate goal by the time we reach the Realms?

The ultimate goal is the specific area in which each of us is to make a unique contribution to the ultimate state.

In considering the ultimate state, I keep getting a jigsaw puzzle picture, each of us fitting into a mass. But I'm sure this won't be it. I should think there would continue to be activity as usual, except that all would be perfect entities of God with each of us doing what we do best for the glory of Creation.

Your idea is not far wrong. It is perfectly true that each of the final goals — which are unique contributions to God's dream — will affect the evolution of the Godhead.

The five goals are:

    to enlighten
    to teach
    to create
    to lead
    to heal.

Is there activity?

Yes. It involves all that concerns relationships, including enlightenment, teaching, creativity, leadership, and healing.

If all is perfect, what need is there for healing, for instance?

This is the only word that comes close to the goal. It has nothing to do with injury or illness of any kind. Rather, it indicates a smoother channel, a cleared way, a harmonious connection in relationships. So it is with all the goals.

As relationships continue to develop in this perfect state, each of us will come to acquire the perfection of all the others. Each gradually takes on the uniqueness of all others, until all individuality is blended into one. Perfect individuality and uniqueness will become one in love in the ongoing evolution of the Godhead.

As more and more souls reach the Higher Realms,

they give loving encouragement to those in the Lower Realms as part of their development process. Those in the First Realm work with the ones in the Place of Preparation as a part of their growth factor, and those in the Place of Preparation strive to influence those on earth. Each higher state administers love and encouragement to those in the lower state. This is a law.

Those in the Highest Realm, who are approaching perfection, make periodic visits to the Place of Preparation and the First Realm, and their very presence has a therapeutic effect on all who see them and experience their presence. They have overcome most obstacles and are looked upon as the "Holy Ones."

You must realize that the names given to the purposes and the ultimate goals here are arbitrary, since it is impossible to truly describe this function in the discarnate world. It is essential, however, to grasp the basic facts to the extent to which it is possible, especially the manner in which they will be utilized when all have reached perfection. The continuing evolution of the state of perfection is an important element of God's plan.

The whole concept of the ultimate state of life is made up of innumerable activities, all designed to bring us into the light of God's Love. At this point you have no conception of what that could mean. But I can say that the ultimate state will be one of complete ecstasy, complete love expressed by all, each in an individual manner. The continuing evolution of life in this state will involve a multiplicity of expression within a spiritual refinement so brilliant and clear as to be utterly transparent. Individuality will be expressed by a frequency that will clearly identify each of us as God variations. Even after each variation has acquired the individuality of all other variations, the entities will always be known by their myriad different individual frequencies.

If individuality, uniqueness, and perfection will all become one as each acquires the qualities of all others, what happens then to uniqueness? Won't we all be identical?

No, certainly not. What you don't quite realize is that the addition of the uniqueness and individuality of all others does not change your own true uniqueness and individuality. Rather, it adds color to the uniqueness of the individuality and expands it in its continuing evolution. The integration of all is essential to the fulfillment of each. But the individuality and uniqueness of each is eternally dominant. One is never mistaken for another. Unique individuality and oneness with God are indeed to be realized, each sharing in the perfection of all others, endlessly evolving. The extent of God's dream is so multifaceted as to be totally incomprehensible to you now. The only reaction possible is to have faith and hope in God's goodness and love for you.

When Christ said "In my Father's house are many mansions," what did He actually mean?

He was referring to the various stages of development within the Kingdom of God — the Higher Realms, each with a separate purpose. Those from the Higher Realms who choose to return to the incarnate world do so to help our ailing civilization. There are many more who return than you suspect. They are the "salt," the "leavening" that gives life to civilization. They come in different ways, but invariably with the same purpose — spiritual advancement. This is always an individual choice, and it may be made from any part of the Realms of God's Kingdom except the First. When the effect of the unique personal individuality is so great that it changes the course of history, it is felt for centuries. A truly advanced soul, a holy one, has come to earth. But many return for love of a certain place or people, to bring about a new concept of a country and government, to originate art or science, or even to rescue someone they love.

Wherever you are you should always keep in mind the realization that God's Kingdom must become present in the incarnate world and He has given you the obligation and privilege of achieving this. You are the elements of God capable of bringing the Kingdom to earth, but if you fail, you are in for a protracted Dark Age when the Kingdom of Self will rule the earth.

Those in the Realms who choose to help by returning can do much toward tipping the scale in favor of construction. But without the cooperation of all of you on earth in seeking construction, they cannot and will not win out. Think about this.

IV. An Overview

The Word is very nigh unto thee
in thy mouth and in thy heart
that thou mayest do it.

Deuteronomy 30:14

I have set before you life and
death, blessing and cursing:
therefore choose life....

Ibid, 30:19

You

How does all of this help us to understand ourselves?
In this overview we are considering you, as the consequence of all you have been.

You must realize that everything you are is the result of all that you have become.

What conclusion am I to draw from that?
Let me tell you a story.

There once was a man who was not what he thought he was. He had always accepted his surface feelings as his primary motivation. He was plagued by compulsion and repeatedly gave into it. However, he also had a loving heart and a generous, giving nature. His compulsions led to drink to dampen the guilt, and his life developed into a continuing cycle of better and worse.

Nevertheless, there was inside this man the possibility of constructive effort and accomplishment of a truly spiritual nature. This was brought out through the intervention of discarnates, and he finally realized his potential after going through a number of trials and proving himself worthy. Such is the story of one man's incarnation including the unseen aspect that brought about an outcome at variance with the expected one.

So it is with each of us. What truly occurs in a life is dependent upon many factors unknown to the casual observer. The success or failure of an incarnation is known truly only to ourselves and our guardians and guides in the discarnate world if we were able to learn, and if not, only to the discarnates.

In other words much of history, personal or historical, is really unknown?

Yes, history is made up of individual behavior, and individual behavior is helped or hindered by constructive or negative forces. This is of the utmost importance to understand so that we appreciate how much help we can receive. In addition, there is never a time when there are not people who come to earth from the Realms to help move comprehension of spiritual matters toward truth for the benefit of humanity. Each of us contributes to the total pattern of God's tapestry. Each individual thread is essential to the ultimate completion of the design of God's choice.

What would you say about the character of the man in your story?

The only element that counts in an incarnation is intention. Once the compulsion was eliminated — even though it took intervention from the discarnates to accomplish — this man's character was then able to function unhampered by karma.

Are you saying that underlying most compulsion there may be real character?

Yes. A person's character is the result of a long period of development over innumerable incarnations. One cannot be judged solely on compulsions, when there are clearly many good qualities also. Compulsions can be temporary, but character is permanent and can shine through when this is made possible.

What can we do to understand ourselves?

Try to look at yourself objectively — the circumstances of your life as well as your elements of development, your purpose, your relationships. Take a bird's-eye view. See what you started with and what you have done with it. Look for the opportunities you have been given.

You can do all that by yourself or with the help of others. But there is one thing only you can do. Try to sense why you came this time. No one else can do that for you. To try to do so for others is misplaced concern. You also must be allowed to make your own decisions and stand or fall on them. This is your privilege and your obligation. Without this choice you would be unable to grow spiritually and build the character necessary to follow God's plan.

How can we know what we have wanted for ourselves in the past?

Your perception of what is important to embark upon now is a clear revelation of the trend of your past desires.

To understand that, your whole nature is to be taken into account. This is essential when determining the balance of power within you. In doing this you are to recognize, but not dwell upon, your faults — just accept that they are there along with much that is good. However, those whose behavior is deterrent and goes unexamined, those who think that what they want and what they need are the same, are the ones who are in the most trouble. Those who do what they want — and want what is constructive — are rare souls, usually advanced souls from the Realms, come to move people along the constructive path.

What is the most important element in life?

The value of your life to God.

What you have become, as a result of all the incarnations you have lived through, is clear evidence of the importances as you have seen them. You are the result of the manner in which you have reacted to all the circumstances and events of your various lives. The value of your life, the value of the eternal you has increased as your efforts toward construction have increased. As you have striven toward a God-willed life, so has your life increased in value to God.

To the degree that you have allowed self-will to enter your life, so you have deterred your spiritual progress and decreased your value to God.

Your value, in spiritual terms is ever-changing, ever-fluctuating in accordance with your own decisions. These changes are expressed in the raising and lowering of the frequency of your spirit. The only way to see yourself clearly is by examining your true heart-feelings. In this way you learn what has importance to you and what you disregard.

What exactly can self-examination tell us?

Although this kind of examination doesn't tell you what you have been through in the past, it can help you determine just where you are at present and whether or not you like what you have learned about yourself. With this knowledge, provided you have been conscientious in your efforts to know just how far you have come, you are able to see yourself in relation to what you hope to become.

God's Grace provides the opportunity to start afresh at any time, to become who you want to be. Any moment of your own choosing can be the beginning of all that you can and will become. No matter what you have done to yourself, no matter what kind of person you have developed into because of what you have done to yourself, you are always able to change for the better at will through the function of Grace. A desire for change is all that is needed.

How is our character built?

Your character has been earned. It is the testimony of what you have been. It is composed of all you retain from all the decisions you have made, all the choices you have preferred throughout your lives, and all that you have done about them. By understanding your character you contribute to your grasp of what is right and what is wrong for you. Your conscience is the essence of your character. The quality of your character indicates what kinds of choices you have made in the past. Character is a sign of growth. A highly developed character denotes strong spiritual growth — and vice versa.

How would you define character?

Character is a person's pattern of behavior, determined by moral strength, self-discipline, and fortitude. It is the aggregate of qualities earned.

What specifically contributes to character?

As I have said, your character is the result of your reactions to all you have been through before; a pattern of behavior determined by moral strength, self-discipline and fortitude.

Your spiritual equipment (love, sense of truth, and intuition), when put to use in the crucial moment of decision, determines what is right and what is wrong, and so contributes moral strength to your character. Character is earned, incarnation by incarnation, each life contributing a specific ingredient. A strong character comes from constructive contributions.

Although self-examination, which helps you to understand the quality of your character, is concerned with your present lifetime only, recognizing what and who you are now gives you the most important clue you have concerning your past lives. You need to concentrate on only one life at a time. Knowledge of former accomplishments or failure could become a harmful preoccupation for most people, although specific knowledge is given to some providing a clue to the reality of reincarnation.

But haven't you said that in the Place of Preparation we will know?

Yes. You will know when you need to. After death you will review this life and all of your previous lives, once you have seen yourself clearly and are preparing to go on. At that time, the knowledge of your past lives can help you to plan the next one and contribute to all the preparation and acquisition that goes into it. At this point, by learning how you have reacted to events in the past, you are enabled to prepare and develop the qualities necessary to improve upon the pattern.

The acquisition of quality is the primary effort of the Place of Preparation. It is exactly at this juncture that you need to see clearly. Proper determination of qualities that will lead to a more constructive life is essential. The choices you make will affect not only the next incarnation but others that follow. A wrong choice here could cause great deterrence in your spiritual growth.

As we look back at our lives, do we see them in the place and time in which we lived?

Yes. It will help you to look at yourself and world history objectively. The rise and fall of civilizations are caused by the return of individuals. The return of great souls — revelers, healers, teachers, scientists, and artists — leavens the whole. The birth of a civilization is the rebirth of an individual soul.

Are you saying that great souls return to cause the fall of civilizations too?

Civilizations run their course, and when it comes time to end them, constructive souls reincarnate to facilitate matters by appealing to souls of moral character to act.

Why?

Because the end of a civilization is determined largely by moral degradation and evil. If a civilization no longer contributes to God's plan, of necessity it must fall to make room for a new one. By the Grace of God, the balance of power is maintained.

The Incarnate World

Please give me a single statement, summarizing the need for incarnate life.

In God's plan for the overcoming of faults and the acquisition of necessary spiritual qualities, the incarnate world was created to offer the opportunity to grow through day-to-day living. The essence of the qualities you need to develop is acquired in the Place of Preparation in the discarnate world. Quantity, however, can be had only through living out an incarnation on earth, putting the quality to use, and, through this effort, eliminating karmic problems, making the quality a permanent part of your spiritual being in the process. Success in this venture is attained only by being properly strengthened in quality, so that you are armed against the possibility of deterrence from without and within.

The incarnate world is the means for implementing God's plan. In the Place of Preparation you are to draw up the blueprints and obtain the necessary material. On earth you are to work to build the structure, constructing from the foundation up, to the best of your ability, hoping to be able to withstand the elements that could cause damage of a deterrent nature or even undo your constructive efforts.

Do we start over again each time?

No. You keep adding to the structure, which remains intact each time. Often as you go along it is necessary to rebuild certain elements that may not have withstood the environment. The intent of life on earth is to create a symmetry of the mental, emotional, and spiritual elements that exist in your lives — these should form a perfect triangle. Those who are dedicated to construction are free to develop the proper balance.

In order to create the perfect triangle with the mental, emotional, and spiritual sides in balance, you must grasp the fact that your spiritual development is dependent upon your mental and emotional response to the circumstances and events of your life. Nothing that happens to us is as important as what we think about it. If you know that, everything that happens is for good, but the good depends upon your reaction to it. You develop constructively in accordance with God's Will and advance spiritually (raise your frequency) in the process. Your spiritual development in the incarnate world depends upon the use of your mental and emotional faculties.

Your heart-feelings are to be utilized in all reactions to circumstances and events through the use of your spiritual equipment (love, sense of truth, and intuition). When the spiritual equipment is unused or misused, the symmetry is thrown off balance and renders you subject to deterrence and prey to Deterrent Force.

This answer seems to imply that mental prowess necessarily increases with spiritual progress, and vice versa. Is that true?

I am using mental here in the sense of the ability to grasp the truth in its essence. We are referring to quality, not quantity. Truly evolved souls may or may not be richly endowed intellectually, but they will always be able to understand and perceive the truth.

What about M. for instance? (A brain-damaged child)
He understands very well. He simply doesn't have the
physical equipment to verbalize it. This could be true
also of coma or stroke. The physical aspect is not included in the triangle.

Supposing there is total brain damage?
With no brain function, there cannot be either spiritual
progress or regression in the incarnate world. Such a
person is in a sort of limbo until life is resumed in the
discarnate world.

*Isn't it true that in sleep we are helped? Wouldn't it
be like that?*
Yes, it is like that. But that does not become real spiritual progress until it can be made real by the individual's own effort.

*Does our intellect continue to function in the discar-
nate world at the level we left off here?*
In essence, yes, but the essence of which I speak is
again the ability to grasp the truth.

*What do we need to dwell on most in the incarnate
world?*
Faith. It is in the incarnate world that the exercise of
faith is put to the supreme test. You must constantly
keep faith in the goodness of God. Once you have rein-
carnated, the curtain is drawn and all of your conscious
knowledge of previous experience and the understanding of how you have coped with the vicissitudes of your
past lives is blocked out. This is purposeful. You are to
learn to trust your heart-feelings, to follow your talents,
and to believe that where you are is where you are
supposed to be. This is not only demanding but also
essential to the outcome of an incarnation. You are

privileged to exercise the faith that directs you toward the constructive path and leads to a fulfilled incarnation. Although it might seem as though more is expected of you than you can deliver, help is always at hand for the asking. In prayer you are realizing the need for help (your true relationship to God) and the humility that that brings about. The beginning of understanding is the acceptance of things as they are.

What will an overview of the world tell us?

History is an unfinished tapestry made up of the threads of all our lives, a subtle interweaving of construction and deterrence.

How do the threads of our lives relate to others?

There should always be a place in your heart for others. As your relationships are interwoven from incarnation to incarnation, so is your contribution to the tapestry of world history. Growth is the essence of relationships. True relationships — those of purpose or blood — must grow. Ignoring a relationship or allowing it to stagnate is as deterrent as broken relationships. You cannot bury a relationship. You must give it a chance to grow.

Who weaves the threads that form the pattern?

All of you are the weavers now. Your lives are the threads. The result of your lives will contribute to the harmony or disharmony of the whole.

This sounds like our various lives, the threads of the tapestry of world history, remain and become permanent. Are we discussing the history of mankind or the development of the soul?

This is important. What you are thinking has validity. However, in order to discuss soul development, we must discuss mankind, since the soul resides in all of us. How we function determines our soul development.

If the threads in the tapestry remain permanent, how do we recognize change?

You are wondering about the wrong things.

The tapestry of history is a record of lives over great lengths of time. As long as there is need for reincarnation, people will continue to exist, and the tapestry will continue to be woven. The tapestry reflects each person's soul development. This is translated into bright or dark threads, reflecting construction or deterrence. Some areas of the tapestry are almost entirely dark. This is because of the development of a dark period in history — a period when deterrence ruled the world. History shows repeated periods of light and dark, whole areas of the tapestry indicating either renascence or dark ages.

What is this all about?

You need to understand that what has been going on for a very long time has importance. All that has happened is recorded so you can see the result of all you have done throughout the ages. You are also responsible for who you will become in the future. History is made up of the reactions of all of us to the circumstances of our lives. We are all responsible for our part in the design of the tapestry, thread by thread.

The Impending Struggle

It seems as though the odds against construction in the world today are insurmountable. Can you give us any hope?

In order to foresee and prepare yourself for the impending struggle, you must understand what is really happening. The struggle is not limited to life on earth, but embraces the seen and the unseen world. It is all one struggle: the Forces of Darkness against the Forces of Light. It is a struggle for the souls of men.

Where does the struggle originate?

It originates in the Will of Self, wherever that may be. It is important to understand that the scope of Deterrent Force is limited by the power available to it. However, now that the power over God's physical universe is being entrusted increasingly to mankind through scientific discoveries, the power that can be appropriated by Deterrent Force is increased proportionately.

Do you mean that the earth is the battleground? Why is this so?

It is the battleground because evil is contained and cannot grow in the discarnate world. It can only increase its power by reaching those on earth.

What good does it do those in the Lower Regions to create havoc on earth?

They gain converts and extend the kingdom of self.

It seems very difficult to believe, although you have already said so, that there are really unseen forces working against us without any conscious awareness on our part.

There are not two sets of rules. If you believe help can be received from God, you must also believe that negative prayers are answered. The concept of immortality presupposes continuing existence. If you give credence to immortality, you are indeed acknowledging that those who once lived on earth are still alive. We are now focusing on those who lived deterrent lives while they were incarnate. What do you think they are doing?

I guess I prefer not to think about them at all. I certainly have difficulty accepting an eternal Hell.

Because you have not understood it as a part of a process — the result of succumbing.

Conceive of human life as a continuum, some of it lived on earth and some of it lived elsewhere. It is all the same continuing life. Those in the Lower Regions can contact deterrants wherever they are, whether it be the Place of Self-Deception or the earth. Those in the Place of Preparation can also contact others within a much higher range of frequency.

Then deterrants here can be helped by those in the Place of Preparation?

They can if they, the incarnates, raise their frequency, which they can do through receptivity; that is, voluntarily acknowledging need and asking for help. It's also possible for those in the Place of Preparation to lower their own frequency in order to help deterrants on earth. Unfortunately, such effort bears little fruit. The likelihood is that with each new wave of deterrence, the gains made would be obliterated.

We have been equating frequency to goodness or spiritual progress. But we have also said that frequency is higher in the discarnate world. How do you reconcile this?

Frequency is in degrees. There is an earth degree and there are different degrees for the Place of Preparation, the Place of Self-Deception, the Lower Regions, and the Realms. Anyone who resides in these various regions has an individual degree of frequency within the frequency of the region itself.

The degree of frequency of the Lower Regions is the lowest in the discarnate world. Nevertheless the degree of earth frequency is lower still. Contact is made through the adjustment of frequency. Deterrants in the Lower Regions can lower their frequency, which is not too far removed from that of earth, in order to recruit those on earth who are vulnerable. This contact is received and perceived as one's own thoughts.

Constructive contact is made from both sides through the raising and lowering of frequency. Incarnates can raise their degree of frequency through prayer and meditation, and also through communication with a guide. Discarnates in the Place of Preparation make contact with those on earth by lowering their degree of frequency sufficiently to blend with the incarnate effort.

Who is organizing this assault on the earth?

The evil geniuses who dominate in the Lower Regions fuel the struggle for souls. They influence whole societies toward evil by seizing power and organizing the Forces of Darkness, pitting their power against the power of the Forces of Light in an effort to gain more and more souls for the cause of world domination.

We've talked a good deal about individual responsibility, but should we on earth be organized to meet this impending struggle?
Individual responsibility fulfilled inevitably leads to co-operation with others. The working out of this is tied to one's goal and final purpose. Christ indicated our differing ways in the Beatitudes, when He not only blessed the poor in spirit and pure in heart, but also the peacemakers and those who hunger and thrust after righteousness.

The power and the ability of Constructive Force is limitless. When this is believed in and acted upon, anything is possible. But faith in the goodness and power of Constructive Force must be unconditional. It requires willingness to take hands off deterrence, to go the whole way toward construction in the knowledge and security that God's Will is good no matter how it may seem.

Isn't there danger that this kind of belief could be purposefully misdirected by deterrants using Deterrent Force?
If you rely on your Spiritual Equipment — your love, sense of truth, and intuition — you will have no problem. Deterrent misuse of faith is always short-lived and collapses in the end, but it is devastating for those who are caught up in it while it lasts. In order to avoid this we must grasp the truth that evil emanates from people in the unseen as well as the seen world. To understand this it is necessary to know the nature of this reality and how it functions.

It seems as though the stakes have been raised — the earth itself and all those on it are at risk.

This present time must be understood. It is a time of disintegration and purification. Sometimes things must disintegrate and return to their basic elements in order to purify themselves. Then new growth will appear. The important thing for all of you now is to distinguish between what should disintegrate and what is being recklessly destroyed. As old values seem to crumble, they will be reborn and revitalized, losing their form but keeping their substance. In both the East and the West, rigid adherence to doctrine must give way so that belief in Christianity and belief in reincarnation may be reunited as they were in the early Church.

Psychics, who work purely and unselfishly to establish constructive communication, will open up knowledge that will give a sense of direction and purpose. The purpose of objective psychic communication is always specific to the time and place in which it happens. As we deal with the impending struggle, there will be a development of information received by psychics worldwide that can unify and strengthen constructive efforts.

The first lesson we must learn is to respect not only ourselves, but Mother Earth, who provides the necessary conditions for reincarnation. We must also recognize that it is only through us that the Forces of Evil can accomplish their destruction.

What is different about the impending struggle compared with our day-to-day struggle for existence?

There is no difference in the kind of struggle. It will, however, become intensified, since deterrence has gained the upper hand and upset the balance of power.

How is this reflected in the world?

Deterrence, which has been a part of us all since the granting of free will, is being expressed at the present time most disastrously through the use of advanced technology. This has the power to deter the process of reincarnation, and bring on periods of darkness that will be devastating to God's plan.

The outcome is up to us. Constructive people, in response to the knowledge of coming events, will be energized and inspired by the great souls who come to help. Those who are dedicated to deterrence will react with anger and fear and will seek to destroy them. Scientists will be among the first of the uncommitted to recognize the validity of psychic communication and to foster the possibility of a new spiritual revelation.

Will it really do good to advocate communication for everyone?

Who would you include or exclude? There is, however, a safeguard. Where there is no talent, a dead end is soon reached. Conversely, talent put to negative purposes will self-destruct in time. Only communication to which the Sense of Truth can respond will last. Communication through thought, meditation, and prayer is available to all.

I can understand the role of the constructive effort because of where it leads. But I don't see the outcome of the deterrent effort. Where do they see themselves residing, since it is all God anyway? How do they overcome the force of reincarnation? Where is their kingdom to be?

First of all, the need of self-will or the Will of Self is self-aggrandizement. Those committed to evil, therefore, try to spread falsehood about the existence of

God. They believe that man is the ruler of the universe and that self-interest is all that matters.

Do they continue to utilize reincarnation?

Once they are committed to evil, they can no longer reincarnate, but, of course, they don't want to either. And the longer they stay, the more entrenched they become. Because of their need to be with others of similar mind, they try to bring incarnates and those in the Place of Self-Deception to their beliefs and their cause — the cause of evil.

Do they see their cause in those terms?

No, certainly not. To them, their cause is the only right one. They see it as the cause of individuality and uniqueness in the service of the Will of Self as they conceive it—the development of the self. You will note that individuality and uniqueness are also the foundation for service to the Will of God. Each side is working for the same development, but for different reasons and therefore with different results.

Since both individuality and uniqueness are elements of the development of the individual toward both the Will of God and the Will of Self, it is easy to become confused about final goals and which of the causes to serve. This is especially true for those of weakened resolve and many karmic problems.

Do you mean that people in general tend to adhere both to the Will of God and the Will of Self?

You are partially correct. What must be clear is that everyone is either deterrent or constructive, but not simultaneously. The attractions of both are evident. Which side one finally comes down on depends upon decisions made from moment to moment and the consequent buildup of either construction or deterrence.

One is induced into construction. One is seduced into deterrence.

As the ultimate state is conceived by both sides is it to be a discarnate state entirely, a combination of discarnate and incarnate states, or is the incarnate state to be primary?

As God Wills it there will be one world only, discarnate and incarnate blended together. However, there can be no final state of self, since it is not a part of God's Will. In the meantime, the Will of Self can disrupt God's plan.

The impending struggle for control over the destiny of man is to be considered in the short term only. Humans have already so polluted the soil, the water, and the atmosphere, that ruination of the world won't take very long at this rate. The job appears to be going on even without the use of the Bomb. Various aspects, such as the hothouse effect, the holes in the ozone layer at the poles, acid rain, despoiling of drinking water, atomic waste, and scientific discoveries that are put to use without knowing the devastating aftereffects, all contribute to causing the havoc that affects not only all life on earth but the process of reincarnation itself.

This seems to be all our doing. Does this kind of deterrence really stem from discarnate involvements?

What you describe may seem to be deterrence caused inadvertently by man alone, but nothing is truly inadvertent. All events are the culmination of the circumstances that have brought them about. Those who see clearly know that all of this deterrence is the result of the interaction between discarnate deterrants and incarnates of weakened moral standards. Incarnate man alone could not create deterrence and evil to this extent.

This is the present state of things. The future will only become worse, unless there is both individual and united action to end this deterrent proliferation. Each of us, in his own way, has a stake in this.

Life on earth is at risk. Although we are using the terms "deterrent" and "evil" in regard to those dedicated to the Will of Self because that is the way they appear to us who have clear vision, they see themselves as the searchers for truth. Dominance of the mind is their goal. They are resolved that through the mind, man can rule the worlds, both incarnate and discarnate.

Both sides see themselves on the right side, and the opponent on the wrong side. The Will of Self utilizes the human mind as the source of its deception. The Will of God uses the human heart (where God dwells) as the source of its revelations. Here we have the fundamental difference in the two forces — one ruled by the mind and the other ruled by the heart. Where the mind rules, God is either set to one side or shut out. But where the heart rules, God rules also.

If God is present in all, can He really be shut out?

When God granted free will, He became a victim of His own decision. Where the mind rules, the self rules, and God's function remains dormant. God is present, but His influence is not felt.

What can be done to right the balance of power?

The forces of construction are being energized by the awareness of incipient danger. The time to prepare is now! It is now that the channels between our worlds can be opened up so that God's Will is felt and known, and those willing to act upon it can be strengthened. That is why we emphasize the importance of each individual becoming a vital channel for Constructive Force.

The dominance of Deterrent Force will continue to

be felt as it is now in every country and every walk of life, and it will grow unless it is counteracted. We are discussing worldwide conditions. The battle must be fought wherever we are, not country against country or people against people, but good against evil, both by diverting the attention from and refusing to yield to, rather than by combatting. The right of the individual conscience must take precedent over the right of law. The difficulties in the Right to Life struggle foreshadow new ethical power struggles created by science, particularly in the field of genetic engineering.

Will this battle be fought on a one-to-one basis?

It will be fought on all levels. We will have the battle of individuals and/or groups on earth standing up against others on moral, ethical, or spiritual grounds — holding out for the wisdom of the heart against all that is put forward in the name of common sense and logic. The conscience of one is ruled by the heart. The conscience of the other is ruled by the mind. Those in the Place of Preparation and those in the Place of Self-Deception and the Lower Regions will also be vying for souls on earth in an extremely intricate and intense manner. The whole matter of who is to dominate the world in the future will be determined by the reactions of both individuals and whole societies to the events of their lives and the forces of stress put upon them. The Forces of Light and the Forces of Darkness in the discarnate world will be struggling for control over the hearts and minds of all who are uncommitted. This is to be a battle of wills, the Will of God against the Will of Self.

Aren't both sides already vying for the souls of the uncommitted in the incarnate world?

The effort is continuous and never-ending, but as long as it is individual and sporadic, it can still be contained.

It would be considered nonsense in your world today to talk or even think about the forces of good and evil as realities vying for the souls of the uncommitted. However, those who are deterrent or evil do not cease to exist after physical death — you cannot wish them away. They are still "alive" and can exert an influence on you from wherever they are. You must take the struggle between those who are trying to harm you and those who are trying to help you seriously.

At what point will this great struggle of wills begin? Since the scale has tipped toward deterrence already, it is imminent. In fact, we already have a foretaste: we see on all sides the evidence of man's doings that stem from self-will and the influence of deterrants. The abundance of lying, stealing, cheating, and deceit among so-called "honorable men" is without precedent. The "religious right" that is trying to impose its will on all is also evidence of blindness to truth. The sovereignty of the individual is being washed away by currents of deterrence stemming from misguided conscience and deceitful moral values. The victimization of innocent people by terrorists, the torture and the killing that fill the news, are the result of the will to dominate the so-called "enemy"—the result of an aberration of the evil mind.

The struggle from the constructive side is to win converts by striving to get them to see clearly. Spiritual blindness is becoming an epidemic. You in the incarnate world have a responsibility to bring yourselves to seeing clearly. Once clarity of vision is achieved, the struggle within us is over for the time being, and we are freed to proceed with the development provided by God's gift of reincarnation. However, constant vigilance is in order, lest we revert. What are you prepared to do?

The Impasse

What can we do, now that we have the power to destroy ourselves?

This a time for realization. A concomitant of the granting of free will was the "expulsion from the garden." Since only God's Will is done in Paradise, the exercise of free will needed to take place elsewhere. A separate world, the incarnate world was created, with the consequence that it gradually become more and more difficult to see or hear those in the discarnate world. The change, though gradual, was absolute. However, the memory persisted for a long time and shaped itself into myths and legends. Great souls — the prophets — could still see and hear, but mankind as a whole lost touch. The great revealers came at different periods to bring us back to a sense of reality, but as the immediacy of their presence faded, so too did our awareness of the other world.

What has this done?

It has caused us to drift from reality into the illusion that our own power is limitless. This has accelerated as scientific discoveries have provided humankind with increasing power. God has granted humans the ability to explore and participate in the physical universe through scientific knowledge. As deterrence seizes and uses this power to destroy and manipulate, it becomes increasingly clear that humans cannot manage alone. Humans have brought themselves to the brink, and it is certain that they don't know what they are doing. The power of Deterrent Force increases with power available to it. At present this is through scientific revelations.

Could you please be more specific?

Scientific revelation, which is intended as a constructive process, can and has become the basis for greater and greater deterrence, as it is made available to those of evil intent. The objective of science is to reveal truth and to utilize the revelations for the betterment of all. However, through the use of scientific discovery of all kinds, deterrence is able to win more and more souls for the Will of Self and world domination.

How do deterrants win souls through advanced technology?

By utilizing the power of technology to influence uncommitted souls toward the worship of technology as man's answer to God. It is easy to believe that man has proven himself "God" on earth through the powers he has discovered and learned to use or misuse. These God-like abilities have proven that the mind of man rules the world! Could God do more? Isn't it reasonable to assume that self-will is the only will worth following? The possibilities of man's will and man's mind are endless! Aren't we Gods after all?

Surely scientific discoveries must also reveal God's plan for the incarnate world?

All scientific discoveries reveal God's plan for the growth and understanding of mankind. When put to use by constructive people, they exemplify the capacity of man to learn and grow in accordance with God's Will, and they reveal, little by little to those of clear vision, God's intent for all and the responsibility to utilize this knowledge constructively. Now, these physical and spiritual powers must be clearly understood and brought into balance by the force of construction.

How could this be done?

By using the spiritual equipment available (love, sense of truth, and intuition), but in this situation, principally love. Even though the balance of power has tipped toward deterrence, the overwhelming power of love could cause constructive harmony to reestablish its power over deterrence and evil and tip the scales heavily on the side of construction.

This would require a mass effort on the part of those who are dedicated to construction. The power of love, expressed by each one, would strengthen construction and help to negate the devastation caused by deterrants. This, in turn, would allow God's plan to develop without extensive delay.

The Whole

What do you mean by, "We are all part of the Whole"?
We cannot separate ourselves. We cannot isolate ourselves. We cannot insulate ourselves. Everything we do affects the whole, just as the whole affects us. Therefore, what happens to us and to the Whole is up to us. Recognition that we are part of the Whole (both worlds) is essential to our development. Seen and unseen, it is all one world. What we do reverberates there and what you do reverberates here. Early man was not cut off from this knowledge. Psychic communication was understood. People understood their dreams. They saw their gods, heard them, argued with them, made covenants with them. And then they wove what they learned into myths and legends, poetry and songs, that enriched and ennobled their lives.

But we seem to have been cut adrift from our source.
Exactly. This early experience was the childhood of mankind, the preparation for emerging self-consciousness. As the self became more identified with free will, and awareness of the other world ceased, the great religions appeared to prepare humans for their new responsibility, pointing the way, reminding them of the dangers, and assuring them of the reality of God and the unseen world. Faith became the cornerstone of their lives. All religions use symbols to give faith vitality. Through the eucharist, Christ left a graphic enduring, visible symbol of man's oneness with the invisible.

But the outcome of our having been cut adrift seems to have been disaster. Was this foreseen?

The danger was foreseen, but was seen as necessary to the solution. The danger made clear the nature of Deterrent Force, so that people, of their own free will, could choose God's Will over self-will and reestablish their bonds to the universe from which they had become estranged.

It would seem then that even Deterrent Force has its constructive side?

You are to look upon Deterrent Force as an element of your maturing process, one that will lead to the knowledge that selfness — self-will, self-concern, self-pity, selfishness, self-servingness, self-aggrandizement — is just a hindrance on the road to recognizing and realizing yourselves as part of the Whole, inevitably linked with all else. This bond places you in proper relationship to all creation as elements of God.

How can we free ourselves from self-concern?

If you know who is in charge, you no longer find it necessary to cling to self because your true nature relates you to the Whole as an essential element of God's Dream. Relationships are the key to understanding your status with the rest of things. There is no longer a need for a sense of superiority or inferiority, because we all are one in God.

What specifically can we do?

In order to arrive at this juncture, there is a difficult job to be done, and you who recognize this are the ones who must do it. The lost sheep must be returned to the fold, and you must start with yourselves. Reincarnation is the method which God has provided for this purpose. Through its function you are enabled to grow and develop. The more you can discover about universal laws, the more ways you can find to work together constructively; the more you can learn about God's Will, the better off you will be. You are part of a great ecosystem, spiritual as well as physical, that is interdependent.

You say we cannot separate ourselves from the Whole. But haven't you also said that those who are dedicated to self-will, deterrence, and evil separate themselves, not only from others but also from God's Will and God's Love? Can you reconcile these two statements?

You must realize that when we discuss what self-will, deterrence, and evil can do, we are talking about the perceptions of the individuals involved. In actuality we are unable to separate ourselves from the Whole because, in the final analysis, we are all elements of God. What you may perceive and what truly exists are often at odds.

How can this be corrected?

Empathy, sympathy, consideration, understanding, are all elements of love, available for the express purpose of bringing our perceptions around to acknowledging the truth that we are all part of the Whole. Nothing is spared in the effort to give us all an understanding of our relationship to all else, and the relationship of all else to us. You must learn never to allow yourself to become dependent upon things beyond your control, because of the drastic effect it can have on the Whole.

Could you explain this more fully?

It is permissible to depend on machines that can improve and simplify the day-to-day vicissitudes of life, but it is not in accordance with the plan to become dependent on chemicals, if the effect continues beyond your control or even your desire to control. Similarly, it is permissible to harness electricity, but it is not in accordance with God's plan to use nuclear energy as long as there is a residue of nuclear waste that results from its development. This waste in itself causes endless havoc with earth, air, and water—all elements of the Whole of which we all are a part. By endangering those elements, you automatically endanger yourselves and the plan for your development. Nuclear power is a grave responsibility. Man is not capable at present of harnessing this power to prevent the disaster that results from its release.

You alone deny the wholeness of the Whole through your acts—a condition abhorrent to God. We are all one in God, and all that you do is paralleled in the discarnate world.

V. Reverberations

The entire universe is governed
by the same laws, differing only
in degrees. Thoughts and actions
initiated in the seen world are
responded to in kind from the unseen.

— From Stephen to Joan and Darby,
The Unseen Guest

Imagination

Acknowledging the interest of all that you have said, what gives it reality? How do we really know?

By the use of your imagination. The imagination, rather than being a somewhat dubious path to escapist daydreaming, can be, in reality, a bridge to the discarnate world.

Isn't it true that my imagination can just as easily be put to evil purposes?

If you are intentionally evil or even deterrent, you are not able to truly imagine. You are merely projecting situations you desire. If your thoughts and daydreams are compulsive, they are not even yours. You are not in control. Deterrence is in control.

It seems to me this is arguable. Where is the line between imagination and desire projection?

The latter is simply an assemblage of images in your mind that arise from your desires. Imagination, on the other hand, frees the mind to function intuitively. It allows you to break through the restrictions of the incarnate world. You give yourself freedom to roam, but you are in control. True imagination will never be put to evil purposes, although it may very well perceive evil, the reality of evil as it exists in both the seen and the unseen worlds.

Everything begins in someone's imagination — every work of art, every scientific achievement, every venture into the unknown. Imagination is the necessary tool for reaching out and discovering what is already there. All you need to do is give yourself permission to say, "What if . . .?" What if life doesn't end here? What if we live forever? What if there is life in another dimension? What if I've lived here before and will again? What if we can reach those on the other side? What if the other side is really right here, but on a higher frequency? What if . . .?

Where will this lead us?

If you will open the door of your imagination wide and contemplate this issue, you will find intuitive feelings coming alive. You may feel peaceful, you may feel a shock of recognition. You may want to read, to talk to others, to pray, to meditate, or to try to communicate in ways new to you. Communication is not an esoteric gift, but natural to all of us to one degree or another.

How are our questions answered?

Answers flood in on those who open themselves to receive! They have given themselves permission to become a party to the creative forces of construction from the discarnate world. They have put themselves in the mainstream of God's creative force and become one with it. In the process, they discover what has not been known before (or has been known and lost or suppressed) and put it into a new context, thus altering the perceptions of humankind. Though they may be regarded as great scientists, great inventors, or great artists, they are actually reflecting what has already been created by discarnates. The time-worn phrase, "God creates, man imitates," is without a doubt the truth. We are all part of the Whole.

I'm afraid I'm put off by the term "imitates." Imitation and imagination seem to me to be at opposite ends of the pole.

The more nearly a work of art, or any other endeavor is like the truth it tries to reach, the more we are moved by it. If an individual is able to subordinate his will to God's Will, his individuality then becomes the medium through which God expresses himself.

I think I understand: it's really a paradox.

Exactly. The hallmark of the quality of a life lived truly imaginatively is your reaction to it. If you are genuinely moved by another's life, if you are changed or transformed by it, you know that the imagination of that soul has been able to penetrate into the unseen world and bring back what it has found.

Please explain the process involved.

It has to do with frequency, which is raised by purpose, energy, and concentration. Those who are truly advanced are able to sustain that effort subconsciously. They live in both worlds at once.

Frequency

*Since you have said all matter has frequency, and
you have defined it as the number of vibrations per
minute, frequency must then be variable?*

The degree of frequency of human incarnate life is not
variable. There is a degree of human frequency just as
there is a degree of frequency for stones, trees, flowers,
different animal species, and so on. Within the human
degree, however, the frequency of every human being
is different from that of every other, and that in turn
varies from moment to moment. You are defined by
your frequency, which includes both your capacity and
your potential, and you are redefined by what you are
doing about it. This is a reality. You know it. You can
feel it in yourself and in others, although it is more
dramatically sensed at both ends of the spectrum. The
frequency of a very developed person, for instance, reverberates through space and time.

*What person are we discussing here, the physical
or the spiritual?*

I will clarify this further.

First of all, let us consider that you have two bodies.
For our purposes these are sufficient. We shall call the
inner body (the eternal spiritual body) the alpha body.
It is the first and foremost body of your concern. The
second or outer body (which varies with each incarnation) we shall call the beta body. It is the alpha body
that decides to reincarnate and inhabit a beta body in
an effort to move forward spiritually through the actions

and reactions of the beta body. Even though the alpha body does continue to function through spiritual equipment, it is entrusting itself to another. What happens in and to the beta body always affects the alpha body in one way or another. The frequency generated by the beta body through its reactions to the circumstances and events of its life affects the frequency of the alpha body in like manner through the Law of Parallels. During reincarnation the growth of the alpha body is dependent upon the growth of the beta body. The raising or lowering of the frequency of the beta body is reflected in a raising or lowering of the frequency of the alpha body. It isn't the actual degree of the frequency of the beta body, but the raising and lowering that affect the alpha body similarly.

Can you relate this to ordinary life?

The frequency you achieve affects your ability to function. Function here is not to be confused with mental prowess or talents, which are given to you as part of your elements of development (the circumstances of your life). By function I mean your ability to develop whatever you have been given through the use of your spiritual equipment, your love, sense of truth, and intuition.

After physical death, your degree of frequency becomes that of your alpha body, as it has now been altered by the frequency it has reached in the life you have just lived.

In other words, when that last life began, the alpha body's frequency was at the level it had achieved prior to incarnating?

Yes. And being spirit, it remains at the level of the spirit world, although it is raised and lowered in accordance with the experience of the beta body.

The experience is at different levels, but paralleled?
Yes.

Would you say then that the achievements of all great scientists, artists, inventors, etc. raise the frequency of their spirits appreciably?
Yes. The importance here lies in the fact that spiritual gain is made through the endeavors of incarnate souls whose efforts reflect the source of all creativity.

What about those whose work certainly does reflect the source of creativity but whose lives do not? Wagner comes to mind here.
In such a case the gift has been earned in other incarnations and has been granted to overcome otherwise very bad karma. The frequency of such people fluctuates wildly.

How will this affect them after death?
They will never be denied the frequency they have achieved. This will enable them to see themselves as they truly are, thereby ushering them into the Place of Preparation. There, they prepare for another incarnation in order to make restitution for all the wrong they have done.

What about the others, those who are both good and great?
They will not reincarnate unless they wish to help right the balance of power by returning to the incarnate world.

Will you please explain frequency in the discarnate world more fully?
All discarnate beings are defined by their frequency. Frequency denotes growth and development. However, here one's development is apparent through quality,

color, aura, etc. What one is, one is. Those who see clearly can determine development at sight.

The ability to see is linked to frequency. The higher one's frequency, the more clearly one sees. Those of a lower frequency see only those in their own degree of frequency, or if they are in the Place of Self-Deception, they can also see those in the Lower Regions whose frequency is still lower. The ability to see is limited by one's frequency. Some in the Lower Regions have such low frequency that they are unable to see.

You mentioned color and aura. How do they function?

I'll give you a rule of thumb. The higher the frequency, the brighter and more radiant the appearance. The lower the frequency, the darker and duller the appearance.

Those in the Place of Preparation are all colors of the spectrum, depending upon their stage and quality of development. Those in the Place of Self-Deception and the Lower Regions grow appreciably darker and duller as frequency lowers.

Can those of low frequency see those of high frequency who come to help them?

In order to be able to help them, those of higher frequency must lower their degree of frequency to match that of the others, just as those who return to earth must take on earth frequency.

How is that done?

In the discarnate world, in order to get on the same "wavelength," so to speak, they must imagine themselves with those of lower frequency. Imagination is essential to deliberately raise or lower the degree of frequency. Because those who choose to help in the

Place of Self-Deception relate to the souls there through imagination, they take on their burden of lower frequency, and are therefore visible to them. However, their efforts are often disregarded; they are looked upon as intruding foreigners. Even so, persistent effort can and does bring results. One spark of desire for change is all that is needed to set construction in motion.

This is not difficult to understand if you think of the great revealers who come back to earth. They assume the degree of human frequency (their beta bodies), while the alpha body retains its own frequency. However, because of their advanced level of frequency, their thoughts and actions are controlled by their alpha bodies, where God dwells. They are thus able to accomplish what they have set out to do, because their higher selves are in charge.

How do time, space, and motion function in the discarnate world?

Here time, space and motion are eternally present. They are in the eternal present. The thought and the place become the same. You ask me a question and I am with you. Your petition has a high frequency because it comes with spiritual intent. All thoughts of love and encouragement are received by all here no matter where they are. To respond, we need only imagine ourselves with you and we are. Our frequency adjusts accordingly.

The Law of Parallels

I feel I don't know enough about the Law of Parallels, how it functions and to what purpose. Would you please discuss this further with me?

You must keep in mind that the Law of Parallels affects all, both those in the incarnate world and those in the discarnate. All deterrent thought, whether it originates in the incarnate or discarnate world, is received by Deterrent Force and reflected back—augmented.

How do deterrent thoughts stemming from the incarnate world, which must have a low frequency, reach Deterrent Force in the discarnate world?

Deterrent Force exists at all of the frequency levels of deterrence and evil. Thought, by its very nature, has a base frequency higher than that of physical matter. Constructive thought has a high frequency. Deterrent thought is much lower, depending on the nature of the thought. However, all thought of any consequence reaches the force to which it is akin, whether constructive or deterrent.

Then both forces exist in the discarnate world?

Yes, you are correct.

Did they originate in the discarnate world?

Constructive Force existed before there was an incarnate world. It is the force of God's Will. Deterrent Force originated in the incarnate world with the deterrent thought of humankind. However the deterrent thought as a force, exists only in the discarnate world. Since thoughts have reality as thought, they are attracted to like thought existing in the discarnate state.

Did the Law of Parallels develop as a result of the granting of Free Will, or has it always existed?

It has always existed. It is one of the laws created by God to regulate the functions of life. Deterrent Force, however, came into existence only as a result of man's misuse of free will. The law is the law and it functions the same way, whether it involves Constructive Force or Deterrent Force.

What about deterrent thought from the discarnate world?

Deterrent thoughts are thoughts that deter God's Will no matter where they come from. The thoughts of those in the Place Self-Deception become part of the body of Deterrent Force. On the other hand, those in the Place of Preparation are using the force of construction to surround the earth with good. It is their pleasurable duty to try to make construction available to all of earth's inhabitants.

What do you mean when you say Constructive Force and Deterrent Force "reside" in the discarnate world?

I mean these forces form the atmosphere in which all discarnates exist. The atmosphere surrounding and permeating those who are deterrent and evil is Deterrent Force. The atmosphere surrounding and permeating those who are constructive is Constructive Force. Although the entire atmosphere of the incarnate world is not affected by deterrent thought, every deterrent person creates deterrent atmosphere. This, of course, is also true of the constructive person. Constructive

Force also surrounds the earth and permeates all those who open themselves to receive it.

Doesn't the force of deterrence also permeate the incarnate world?

No, not in this way. What you see around you are merely acts of deterrence and evil by incarnates victimized by deterrants using Deterrent Force.

Even so, I should think it capable of permeating earth's atmosphere.

No, it is not. This is against God's Will.

Is everything we think and do paralleled?

Yes. Just as every natural law is paralleled in the two worlds, so every thought, action, and emotion is responded to. Every constructive or deterrent thought or action in the incarnate world raises or lowers the frequency of an individual's spirit, thus creating a closer affinity to the discarnate world. Construction raises frequency, bringing one closer to positive forces. Deterrence lowers it, making one vulnerable to negative forces. This is a law. It is not the actual frequency but the raising and lowering of it that brings on the result. Raising frequency reflects aspiration. Lowering frequency reflects degradation. It is automatic. It is the reason why energy is created spontaneously from positive efforts.

This principle carries all through life, so that the constructive one does things of increasing difficulty with increasing ease, whereas the situation is reversed for the deterrent one. Just as the residue of negative thought and actions poisons the atmosphere — a phenomenon that can actually be felt — so constructive thought and action energize the atmosphere — which can also be felt.

The need to become one with God lies deeply within us all. It is an important part of our fundamental makeup. But it often takes deep self-examination to uncover this fundamental need of our being, and to realize that construction is at the root of the energy it takes to do it. The difficulty is in getting started. But once we have accomplished that first dead-lift, a cycle of energy and renewal of energy, resulting from the Law of Parallels, leads to greater awareness of the existence of the unseen world and the hope that emanates from it.

Please explain more fully how the law functions.

Constructive thoughts and actions are magnetically attracted to Constructive Force, which is the force that develops from each thought and action, whether incarnate or discarnate, that is in harmony with the Will of God. Deterrent thoughts and actions are magnetically attracted to Deterrent Force, which is the force that develops from each deterrent thought and action from either side that is in league with the Will of Self.

Do you mean that any thought or action no matter where it originates is paralleled on the other side?

You see, the incarnate and discarnate worlds are one universe. Any thought or action becomes a part of reality. It therefore exists. That reality, if it is deterrent, becomes part of the deterrent world. If it is constructive, it becomes part of the constructive world. What do I mean by deterrent world? I mean all of negation, whether discarnate or incarnate, and the atmosphere in which it exists.

But is the paralleled response specific?

It is always specific, a specific response to a specific thought or action. What you are really asking is whether it is personal. It can be. If so, it is usually because someone in the discarnate world is close to the situation and concerned, whether positively or negatively.

Didn't you say there is no communication from the deterrent world?

Conscious communication with the discarnate world must be understood as a function of the Spirit of Truth only. A parallel response from the deterrent world comes from invading the atmosphere with a maelstrom of negative vibrations, so that those who are vulnerable get sucked in — "For they have sown the wind and they shall reap the whirlwind."*

Aren't we talking about a specific response from a specific place? For instance, prayer. We don't feel as though we are just sending our prayers out generally. We direct them.

Constructive prayer becomes a part of all of reality, and all of reality benefits from it. However, it is also true that those whose development has raised their frequency so they are able to penetrate the discarnate world, such as some psychics and mystics, can bring about positive and even miraculous specific response.

Should we think of place or of higher and lower frequencies, or do they interpenetrate?

Think of them as the same thing. We speak of "Place of Preparation" and "Place of Self-Deception" metaphorically, for reasons of simplicity. It is not the purpose of this communication to go further. The Law of Parallels operates as a raising or lowering of frequencies.

---

* Hosea 8:7.

I can see how positive thought and action can raise my frequency here, but how is that paralleled in your world?

By a corresponding raising of frequency on this side, which is directly beneficial to the one who has brought it about.

If I were to make a good enough effort in regard to this work, how, specifically, would the law work?

You would have raised my frequency, from which you in turn would benefit directly.

Whose frequency would be raised were there not an established relationship?

The frequencies of all here who are associated with the one there, but specifically, anyone particularly involved in the effort being made.

If this results in a lowering of frequency in the case of negation, how is that paralleled?

In exactly the same way: instead of raising, it lowers, or pulls the one on earth farther down.

So that I understand this fully: are you saying that constructive thought raises the frequency of the person thinking?

Yes.

Are you saying that this thought, which we understand contributes to Constructive Force, also affects those on the other side?

Yes.

Just who would they be?

They would be all those who are involved with the development of the individual on earth, his guardian angel, his guide, his loved ones who are discarnates.

Would constructive thoughts also affect those incarnates who are close to the individual here?

Yes. The atmosphere of construction affects all who are within the specific sphere of influence.

Does it raise their frequencies?

Yes, it does.

Do we carry our degree of frequency with us from incarnation to incarnation?

Yes, we do, and also we can add to it during our stay in the Place of Preparation.

Intensifying frequency in order to reach our ultimate goal must be a very slow and arduous process.

It is. It takes endless time and effort to finally reach perfection.

Please explain what the Law of Parallels means to us in our daily living.

It means that you are part of a Whole. It means reinforcement. It means that whatever you do, good or bad, comes back to you. It is the simple routine of daily life — "as you sow, so shall you reap." It means that prayer is answered, constructive effort brings results. It means also that deterrent thoughts and acts bring about their own consequences. How is this implemented? What exactly happens? The parallel response is in proportion to the intention and energy expended, good or bad. Energy that is concentrated and directed is felt and responded to in the unseen world. Conversely, energy in the unseen world that is concentrated and directed is felt and responded to in your world.

This is not, however, to be confused with mind-reading or telepathy. It's simply that the energy of my thought and intention sparks the energy of your thought and intention, and vice versa. It has nothing to do with communication. That is an altogether different matter. Similarly, evil thoughts, for instance, the thoughts and schemes of a terrorist, spark the energy of Deterrent Force in a way that is stimulating to those deterrants in the discarnate world who are responsive to that particular quality.

Will you help me to understand this more precisely?
The entire universe has one consistent set of laws. All the laws with which you in the seen world are familiar are paralleled in the unseen world and vice versa.

Within this framework, it is also true that any action taken in the seen has a parallel reaction in the unseen, and vice versa. It therefore follows that any action for good or for evil in the seen is greatly augmented by a parallel action in the unseen and vice versa.

Constructive Force, having existed from the Beginning, originates in the unseen. Whereas the potential for Deterrent Force became a reality only after man was granted God's privilege of choice, free will. Deterrent Force therefore originated in the seen world. The growth of a tree in the seen parallels the law contained in the thought of the growth of a tree in the unseen. All that is thought or conceived here can be paralleled by those of you here who can conceive and reconceive within the limits of the degree of law there. The word usually associated with this process is inspiration. If we describe a person as an "inspired" leader, or musician, or prophet, even the layman understands that he has received his gift from a source outside of himself. What one receives and what one returns depends upon one's own development.

What are the important elements of this subject?
The key element involved has to do with the way people think. Not only are they affected by their

thoughts — constructive or deterrent — but the thoughts themselves generate a similar response that augments the original with the same energy, greatly increased. In this way, the end result of a thought creates a much more powerful effect than the thought as originally conceived. It's like seeing your face in a magnifying glass. The original becomes greatly magnified in the process.

No matter how slight you may regard your criticism of another person, even if it is only a thought, that thought is reinforced from the discarnate world. Although it can affect the other person to a degree, it is much more damaging to you. If this thought is expressed verbally it also has a damaging effect on the one against whom you express your criticism.

You are in no position to judge others, no matter how well you feel you know them (including members of your own families), because, even in such intimate relationships, you cannot know the true situation of another soul. The internal spiritual life of others, which is the source of their actions and reactions, their thoughts and motivations, their karma and understanding of their lives, are closed to your inspection. What you see is merely an outward manifestation of an inner being. Judgment of others is odious because it is never based on the true facts, only on what appears on the surface.

There is one point I'd like you to bear in mind. All constructive thought comes from aligning yourself with Constructive Force, which permeates your world from this side. Whenever you respond to the forces of construction that come to you from outside, you cause them to reflect back. What you do that is constructive is always in response to the effects of the construction that surrounds you. The channel of construction is open to all of you and you partake of it as you will, growing spiritually, thus raising your frequency more and more in the process. What you think and do that is constructive is yours and comes from opening yourself to receive the Constructive Force that envelops you from our world.

All accomplishment is achieved by the aligning of oneself intuitively and imaginatively with the Constructive Force that is the source of all creation, and assimilating that which has already been created in the discarnate world, in order to bring it to the incarnate world.

Communication

Constructive Communication

How would you define communication?

Communication is not the Law of Parallels, and it is not intuition — both of which are universal. Nor is it answered prayer. It is a gift possessed by all of us to some degree. However, when true psychic ability manifests itself to an unusual degree, it is a special talent that is part of the elements of development. It manifests itself in individuals for a purpose related to that person's goal. If it is used for wrong purposes, the result will be evil. Those who cheat or use it to their own advantage will have a karmic price to pay. But if those whose purpose is objective enlightenment will maintain faith and diligence, they will be able to open communication between the two worlds as true messengers of God.

What is my protection? Supposing I think I am doing my very best to be honest, how do I really know?

This will prove itself out in time. Time and effort are important factors. You may go through many trials, but if you grow in strength and character and serenity in spite of them, you know you're on the right track.

You should regard as negative any unwanted intrusion of thoughts, any temptation to use your communication selfishly, any feeling of uneasiness, any expectation that your problems will be solved for you.

It seems to me some of those negative things occur as trials and tests.
That's true, but your honest recognition of them dispels them.

I suppose the best way to know if the material received is true, is if construction results?
Communication that is truly constructive may appear to many to be ridiculous. One can only rely on one's own sense of truth, wherever it may lead. If you do this, you will grow in love and strength and character.

On the other hand, those who are reached by deterrants are not necessarily evil. They may be confused because they refuse to recognize the existence of evil. This comes from a lack of understanding of free will. Or they may simply be seeking instruction or predictions regarding day-to-day problems for themselves or others.

This kind of communication is seldom productive, because you are then robbing the sense of truth of its function. Generally speaking, those who communicate get what they deserve. Those who trivialize this gift receive trivial or misleading answers. Even after an answer appears to have been received, it is impossible to know what source the answer came from or why it was received. This is why the use of the Ouija board or other similar means may lead to disaster, to amusement, or to a life of dedicated work, depending entirely on the purity of intention with which they are used. If the sense of truth has been reached there is a shock of recognition that tells you this is indeed reality. If this is your purpose, if this is what you came to do, you will then start out to live a new life of dedicated, concentrated training.

Will communication become convincing evidence of the reality of your world?

Through trained receptive minds emptied of ego, we are able to bring about a condition wherein the two worlds are functioning together. When this happens material can be conveyed that will strike some as true. This will not become a movement. It will be the work of individuals here and there giving and receiving, in their own ways, aspects of the truth concerning the interrelationship of the worlds. This will in time help constructive souls to pursue their own goals for the betterment of all. Many do this now because they come well prepared and are not confused about why they have incarnated. In time many others will also learn to trust the inner voice, the means by which truth is transmitted to all of us, and yet is personal to each one of us.

I understand that if we're honest with ourselves we can rely on our Sense of Truth, (our inner voice), but that true communication is more difficult.

Inaccuracy is inevitable. It isn't that the material is not received, but that it is not listened to with enough concentration. The quality of this work can vary, just as it would if you were taking notes at a lecture. Mistakes are only too ordinary and human. If you are too tired, you can always resume at another time. There can be, however, no uncertainty of purpose.

Do you think most people believe in your existence? Very few people can accept the reality of communication.

I think they do intuitively. They pray, they curse, they bless each other when they sneeze, they consign their enemies to hell. It's just that putting the ego aside and really listening is so much harder.

Are simple activities such as the Ouija Board and automatic writing constructive demonstrations of communication between the two worlds?

They are in themselves neither constructive nor deterrent. This depends largely on the purpose for which they are used. Since they require little more than an open mind, they can be useful first steps toward serious psychic communication. However, because of the low level of frequency required, deterrence may interfere. If no purposeful communication develops, if replies are senseless, obscene, irrelevant, or offensive to one's sense of truth, or if nothing at all happens, one should not attempt to continue.

Are our loved ones in the unseen world able to help us? Is it wise to try to reach them?

Yes.

Tell me about how we should think of them. What should our thoughts be?

For one thing, never convey negativism, grief, or sadness of any kind. If you direct your thinking toward individuals with love, faith, and hope, they will receive your thoughts and benefit from them. Praying for their welfare and asking them to pray for you results in benefits on both sides, even though there may be no conscious response. Also, you will benefit, as will they, from their thoughts directed toward you if you open yourself to receive. When this happens, you will notice an energy, an exhilaration, filling your being as a result. This is the Law of Parallels in action.

This is communication on a simple level; it is open

to all with no previous preparation. This form of communication could be more rightly called meditation. The important element here is to believe without doubt in the reality of your loved ones in the discarnate world, waiting and wanting to hear from you. In this instance it is emotion that is being transferred back and forth. The emotion is love — the balm that heals all wounds, both emotional and spiritual.

What about actual communication?

It is important to realize that many have the ability to communicate and intercommunicate without acknowledging it or perhaps even realizing it. Fear is the most common reason for this. One tends to fear the unknown and doubt what cannot be proven. However, if you give yourselves the freedom to try, and if your intention is pure, you may embark upon a real adventure. You may well be tempted to ask foolish questions. If so you will probably be tested by the foolish answers that result. Your credulity may be strained, but if you remain objective and steadfast, you may gradually realize that you have a job to do — a job other than your regular workaday and family life, which should be maintained in a normal manner. This part of my message is meant for those who relate to it. They sense who they are. There are many serious, rewarding jobs to be done, many roads that need to be opened. Many have done this and are doing it, but now there are to be many more.

What if one is not satisfied with just thinking about loved ones on the other side and would like to learn to communicate?

Those who are interested should not attempt this work without the realization that it is a long and often discouraging discipline, which must permeate but not interrupt the ordinary flow of life. The aid of a person who is knowledgeable about these matters may help them to get started, showing them methods and explaining problems that they could face. However, you should not attempt communication, unless you feel strongly that this is a serious venture. It is not for those who just want to be titillated by the experience. For many, prayer and meditation alone satisfy their needs and fulfill their hearts desires.

Working with a discarnate spiritual guide, with the intention of furthering understanding and increasing the ability to live from moment to moment constructively, can be rewarding beyond one's present comprehension. In seeking this, there is a fundamental principle to be considered: water seeks its own level. Those whose interest is surface or selfish will be drawn to others of like mind. Those whose true purpose is communication will be led into the right circumstances for them.

If you are ready and willing, you will be given the help you need, whether it is from incarnate or discarnate sources. You should respond to the circumstances that are given to you. This work will chart its own course, depending upon your needs. Faith and trust, coupled with obedience to the Will of God, which is represented by one's spiritual guide, are essential ingredients to success.

What else besides obedience is required?

Fundamental to the development of any psychic gift is purpose. If your purpose is to reach out to us in friendship, trust, and love, you will be rewarded. The Law of Parallels applies here without fail. If your purpose is frivolous, the result will be frivolous. If it is deterrent, the result will most certainly be deterrent. If it is objective enlightenment, the result will be just that. There is no way Deterrent Force can harm those who do psychic work if the purpose is pure and if the channel of communication is never misused or abused. It will be protected and kept inviolate from interferences as long as it is used to ascertain truth.

But what about those who do experience interference?

Interference is a clear sign that all is not well. Psychic activity should cease, allowing time to recognize why deterrants were able to enter the channel, and to correct the condition, which may be spiritual, intellectual, or physical.

Is there a certain way to recognize interference from deterrent sources?

It is often unintelligible, disjointed, alarming, or seductive. The purpose may be simply to destroy confidence in the divulgence being received. It should never be allowed entry. Simply close the door and wait for a time of more concentrated energy and purpose. Psychic communication can be very dangerous for those who use it to their own advantage, to influence others, or try a short-cut through drugs or other means. It must be allowed to grow in accordance with one's own spiritual development.

Never try to escape the routine burdens and demands of daily life through this means. They are necessary for development.

I would like the business of purpose clarified. Purpose implies that specific results are required from the effort. What should they be?

If we are discussing some form of active communication with someone special on the other side, we are involving two souls, one incarnate and one discarnate — you, and someone who is known and loved perhaps, or maybe someone who is interested in helping in some way. Through this process, spiritual knowledge that can affect many many people constructively can be conveyed — truth as it is clearly seen on the other side. From this communication much can result. The incarnate partners on earth can be helped to understand their problems and goals more fully. They can learn much about the purpose of life itself, but more particularly about their purpose in reincarnating this time around. They may even, perhaps, learn just who they are and where they are headed, and how to live each day to best advantage, in the hope that these truths will take root. If such people find themselves drawn to the truths in these teachings they also may discover that there is some form of communication that is right for them, the pursuit of which could mean their salvation.

Although it may be possible to recognize your faults (your karmic problems that must be overcome in order to qualify for God's plan for you), it is entirely beneficial and edifying to seek to learn about them in first-hand communication. This leaves no doubt as to their reality, nor as to the necessity for eliminating them. Even though pride may be considered indigenous to human nature, it is humiliating and sobering to accept all of one's other faults as well.

If and when you have established a deep, clear channel of love, you begin to realize the unique opportunity you have to learn all you need to know to satisfy God's plan for you. The privileges and responsibilities this knowledge grants you can be overwhelming. As your purpose this time is made crystal clear, and you gain an understanding of how this ties in to your ultimate goal, the seriousness of this endeavor is impressed upon you in a way that allows for no escape. If you want to follow God's Will for you and become one with Him, you realize the necessity of dedicating yourselves to construction and the need to resolve your problems in order to do your share in combatting the rapid growth of deterrence.

This all sounds so simple and idealistic, and yet it seems there is great variation in the context and quality of the work received by genuine psychics. Why is this?

This is important to understand, so that those embarking on this field are not discouraged. Because psychic communication must be filtered through the brain of the recipient, it is not possible to totally bypass the thought patterns already there. It is also not possible to find ways of expressing thoughts foreign to the recipient's comprehension. But just as we are limited by you, you also are limited by us. The individual from whom you may receive undoubtedly has a particular intention and point of view. For instance, even though I can and do work in consultation with others here, the information I receive from them is limited by my capacity and point of view, just as the information you receive from me is limited by your capacity and your questioning mind.

However, no one in the Place of Preparation could or would communicate an untruth except as a means of teaching (testing), in which case the recipient can't be harmed, but will learn. Any communication that develops will reveal the spiritual authority of the sender. It will therefore be more fully experienced and have a lasting effect. The most important factor is relationships. The quality and kind of material received is to some extent determined by the relationship between those communicating. Beyond that there is purpose and method. The method used, for instance, with Stewart and Betty White differs from the method used with Edgar Cayce, and this in turn has to do with the purpose to be accomplished.

It is therefore wise for those who embark on psychic work to allow for a long, slow period of development, so that the method and purpose can reveal themselves in accordance with the effort and steadfastness of the recipient.

Deterrent Communication

What if we get mixed up with deterrants?

It is important to understand that true communication can only take place with the constructive discarnate universe. By "communication," for the purpose of this dialogue, what I mean is the exchange of truthful thoughts—this means truthful on both sides, yours and mine. The reason there must also be truth on your side is that we cannot answer if your motivation in asking is not honest. The question may not even come to us; it could be intercepted by deterrants.

Can this happen without our realizing it?

Any questions that are self-serving run this danger, even though they may seem innocent to you. This is inevitable, as you well know, in the early stages of communication. It takes years of training to become sufficiently objective to build a secure channel.

I can see that communication, as you define it, isn't possible between negative forces, but doesn't some kind of communication take place?

Reciprocal communication is contrary to the nature of deterrence. Those in the discarnate world who have become encased in self, who are unable to function outside of self, are therefore incapable of seeing or relating to the Whole. As far as they are concerned, they are the whole. All else is an extension of themselves. Therefore their chief concern is to enforce their will. Deterrent Force, the energy of the evil intent resulting from this, is a reality that reaches those who are vulnerable.

The only thing to which the deterrants can really relate is the strength and power they once had on earth. Therefore, they try to recreate it by concentrating on deterrence and evil. The virus of evil thus becomes manifest in individuals and infects whole societies, using individuals as carriers of Deterrent Force. This is often true of those with psychic ability. Others of weakened will are easily influenced by them with disastrous results for everyone, especially the psychic. On the other hand, psychics who are dedicated to truth can decipher the efforts of deterrants and have nothing to fear from them.

Is it a good idea for those who do not have a pronounced psychic gift to go to those who are so gifted for advice and help with their lives?
Provided they go with an open mind, alert to their own sense of truth and intuitive feelings; even then, it is well to put the advice on a back burner and see what happens. If the psychic has been able to be truly helpful, the likelihood is that developments will begin to present themselves.

Might that also be true if deterrent psychics took the initiative?
The same principle applies throughout. The answer you receive will be in accordance with your intent in asking. There are many false prophets—many, in fact, who do not recognize this themselves. Cynics who know they are fakes are far less dangerous than those who are convinced of their own "divinely ordained" mission.

Some who start out as true psychics gradually, through pride, turn it to their own selfish advantage, and in so doing become subject to Deterrent Force. The result can be extremely subtle and dangerous because it can represent a mixture of truth and lies. If such psychics can be persuaded by deterrants that the communication is from God, they are both powered by their own conviction and victimized by it. In time this madness will burn itself out.

The result, however, is that many come to fear psychic power itself. This is unfortunate because the potential for good is so much greater than the potential for evil. Evil will inevitably disintegrate; it cannot renew itself. It must be fed. Whereas good, nourished by the power of God, is capable of infinite growth.

That being the case, why are we in so much trouble?

It is not from psychic communication; not even from the misuse of psychic communication, which has actually played a very small part in the history of civilization. The problem is much more the lack of understanding, not just of the possibility of psychic communication, but of all that this implies — the oneness of all of life, seen and unseen, and the astonishing potential it offers for the improvement of life on earth.

Will that understanding come about?

I would say that is the intent of the future.

What do you mean by that?

No one can predict the future accurately. The most constructive efforts can result only in seeing the intent of the future, never the event itself. A clairvoyant may see the possibilities, but since the actuality depends upon both the reactions of those who are involved and the subsequent resultant circumstances, the actual event is the result of all that goes before it and cannot be predicted with absolute accuracy. Circumstances alter events. It is possible, of course, that the intent does indeed become the event because everything has turned out according to plan. But this remains an unusual circumstance and cannot be predicted accurately.

What about a sense of immediate disaster?

Such a sense or feeling or premonition has more validity because of its immediacy. The long-range prediction is more complex and therefore more difficult to achieve.

If I am an evil person and I want to cooperate with evil discarnates, can I not ask a question and receive an answer?

Yes, of course you can. But that is not true communication. The answer your receive is what the other person wants you to hear. This is because you would both be speaking from your own self-interest.

But supposing our self-interests coincide?

That could not be true unless you're willing to surrender your self — in which case you would have "sold your soul to the Devil." You would have separated yourself from God's Will.

From what you say it sounds as though communication is not for everyone.

Communication in the broader sense — belief in the reality of the unseen world, and belief in the good and the harm that can come from it — is certainly for everyone. Many people are open to this belief but are put off by charlatans and the misuse of psychic ability. This will change as dedicated psychics try to receive truly. Messages will be very different for the reasons familiar to you, but that is because there are many ways to understand the same truth.

The good that will come will be brought about through helping people understand how important and meaningful their lives are, and through providing an incentive to live in accordance with their own intuitive feelings. As life begins to make sense and you understand why you are here, you are freed to be yourselves.

Science and the Unseen

Isn't it true that the conditions of life on earth limit our perception of the unseen world?

No. It is true that conditions of life on earth are needed for spiritual growth, and that spiritual growth is necessary to perceive the unseen world.

Does this mean that the unseen world cannot be revealed by scientific means?

It means that a true comprehension of what is discovered by scientific means cannot be attained except through spiritual growth. Those scientists who understand the interdependence of life on earth and work to extend that point of view will eventually find themselves on the threshold of the unseen. If you keep your eyes straight ahead you will see the horizon — the point where the two worlds meet. That is a symbol, of course, but symbols are images of reality.

This doesn't sound like the detached scientific point of view. Why would one's attitude affect what one learns?

Because acceptance of oneself as a part of a whole necessarily entails respect for the Whole as well as a willingness to accept rather than project. Great scientific breakthroughs, like great art or great revelations, come about when there's a unity of purpose between the worlds. When psychic and scientific work finally find a common ground, it will become clear that all of us in the universes in which we live are one.

Will it be possible to see the unseen by scientific means?

Yes, this is already possible. Many have seen Kirlian photographs of auras radiating from the fingertips of healers and from plant leaves. There is, however, a wide variation in attitude and belief toward what is revealed. While doubting Thomases may be convinced of life after death once science makes it apparent, this knowledge alone will not change their hearts. There will be those who fear this knowledge, those who seek to exploit it, and those who will try to destroy it.

Remember there are two kinds of "seeing." Seeing with the physical senses or an extension of them through scientific means is one—a most valuable one to be developed and explored indefinitely. But there is also inner seeing—the understanding of the heart. Both are voyages of discovery, and to some extent both are triggered by the imagination. We may not be able to imagine what we finally discover, but we must at least be able to imagine that there is something to be discovered. Just as in our ordinary lives we sometimes stumble upon an unplanned discovery, so does the spiritual seeker.

Spiritual serendipity.

It happens all the time.

Are deterrants able to subvert this?

To some extent, particularly within the scientific community itself. But the compelling nature of the revelations supporting interdependence will build an overwhelming momentum.

Will it be possible to prove your existence through scientific means?

Yes, but before it becomes possible, it must be imagined to be possible. The Law of Parallels must be understood.

Psychics can help scientists to understand that for every law governing the seen world there is a parallel law governing the unseen. By extending the laws of your universe as far as they can go, you could prove my existence — even the existence of realms beyond this one — but that would not give you the power to function beyond your own world. The means for proving the existence of something does not give you the powers inherent in that existence. That cannot happen without the transformation that occurs at the death of the body, which frees the spirit from incarnate life.

Exactly what is it that will be gained by greater scientific knowledge of life after death?

It is the knowledge that we live in different facets of one universe; the certainty of reincarnation and immortality; reinforcement of the idea that life is a continuing process and that therefore the way in which we live our lives on earth has very serious consequences. The gradual acceptance of this knowledge will have a decisive effect in righting the balance of power.

VI. The Practice of Faith

It is through the practice of faith
in the Love of God that man is enabled
to live a constructive life, fulfilling
his responsibility to eliminate the evil
he has caused and bringing God's Will
to earth.

R.

Prayer and Self-Sacrifice

How does prayer fit into the concept of communication?

Prayer, in its most profound form, achieves union with God's Will. In such cases, the prayer itself is its own answer. All constructive prayer is an effort to unite our own forces in the direction of good. It is an act of love. It embraces our deepest relationship, that with "Our Father." By asking for help, we create within ourselves that receptive state of mind needed to bring about a change in ourselves and in the world.

Is this true of all prayer?

No, it isn't. Not all prayers are constructive. Those that are self-centered go no farther than the Kingdom of the Self. This provides a means through which Deterrent Force returns to Earth. There are no unanswered prayers. That is why we say, "Be careful what you pray for. You may get it."

How can we be sure our prayers are constructive?

The "Our Father" forms a model for all prayer. It defines our relationship to God, our place in the universe, our legitimate expectations, our obligations. "Lead us not into temptation" defines the opportunity and the gravity of self-will, so we can of our own free will resist temptations (meet the test) and become one with God's Will. And finally, it provides the solution: it is God who can deliver us from evil. We are delivered from evil when we accept God's Will because Deterrent Force becomes powerless when it loses its ability to control.

Of what should prayer consist?

The important elements are praise, meditation, and thanksgiving.

Of what should praise consist?

Praise involves your relationship to God. By praising God's glory, power, and majesty, you are confirming the completeness, the wholeness, the All-in-Allness of God and acknowledging your relationship to the Whole. You are expressing humility and clarifying the necessity for obedience to the all-powerful, all-loving being-God.

What exactly is meditation?

This is primarily contemplation that often results in a one-sided conversation. In old-time religion it was (and still is) called talking to God. In this way you are expressing your faith, your love, and your need for God's goodness and your trust in God's Will for you. In a meditative state, you examine these thoughts and allow them free rein. You ask for guidance in your daily life toward achieving your goal. You ask for help in understanding your problems and the purpose they serve. You pray for the welfare of your loved ones in both worlds and for their spiritual progress. You ask for the understanding and strength it takes to live a constructive life. You ask for forgiveness for your misdeeds. This might be called active meditation, in contrast to more passive forms of meditation such as those practiced in Eastern religions.

Please clarify what you mean by thanksgiving.

The thanksgiving is a whole-hearted expression of gratitude to God for all of the blessings bestowed upon you. You count your blessings and you express yourself in the terms that most explicitly define them. You recognize the source of all the lessons being taught you in one way or another. You acknowledge your need for them and your gratitude for what they have taught you. You thank God for the privilege of incarnate life with all its opportunities and its pitfalls so that you can continue to grow and to learn until, with God's help, you finally have realized the potential with which you were created.

What is the meaning of the Cross?

The meaning of the Cross is that we all must suffer before coming to true fulfillment. We must suffer the consequences of our karmic problems. Suffering is part of growth. Fulfillment is the result of effort. Suffering and effort go hand in hand as the prerequisites of fulfillment. God shares with us the suffering we brought upon ourselves by bringing about evil as a result of self-will. It is through the acceptance of suffering that we can share with Christ in overcoming that evil.

What significance has the Cross for us?

When Christ said, "pick up your cross and follow me," He said "your cross." You all have crosses to bear. These crosses are the problems you have given yourselves, your karma. The circumstances of your lives are there for a reason. By responding to all events with faith, hope, and love, you are proving yourselves worthy of the faith God has in you. You are reacting constructively to the testing each event presents. You are not to impose difficulties on yourselves just to prove your worthiness. This will be accomplished by the circumstances and the events that follow upon your choice of parents and by following the guidance of your hearts. Your development is proven by your reactions to events within your relationships. If you react constructively, no matter how difficult that may be, you are proving yourselves and improving yourselves at the same time. By assuming responsibility for the elimination of your karma, you are indeed picking up your crosses and following Him.

What is meant by "follow me"?

It means that you must view and accept all that happens to you in the right light. The events of your life must be lived out in faith, trust, and humility, knowing that God loves you and wants only good for you. If you live in this manner, giving up your will, you are contributing construction to the circumstances of your life. Construction lies at the base of all events. Through construction your wills and God's Will mesh. There is inevitability to all events depending upon how you react to them, either toward construction or toward deterrence.

What do you mean by giving up my will?

I mean the act of self-sacrifice. By self-sacrifice we mean giving up self-will for God's Will. It is in this way that God becomes manifest on earth. The power released through the Cross is as real today as it was two thousand years ago. All acts of selfless love and service contain the seed of life, and will therefore grow, even though it may appear that Deterrent Force has won. Understanding and believing in the continuation of life allows you to see things as they really are, and helps you make the difficult choices. You recognize that only by being self-less can you ever really be both individual and whole.

Individuality

How can we sacrifice self and still retain individuality?

Self-sacrifice does not mean sacrificing individuality. You are a unique individual. You were so created. The potential inherent in an individual may be developed or undeveloped, but it remains nevertheless. It is eternal. It is you. The development of that individual potential is what we call character. Personality, on the other hand, is a gift. It is part of our elements of development and varies from incarnation to incarnation.

If individuality is neither character nor personality, what is it?

This has to do with final goals — the capacity of a newly created individual to fulfill a unique job that can be accomplished by no other individual. This capacity is its individuality. When you sacrifice self-will for God's Will, you are not sacrificing individuality. On the contrary, you are enabling your individuality to express itself.

In what way?

By allowing your individuality to identify with the Source and thereby express the God in you. If your individuality can be a minute expression of the Will and Love of God, you are fulfilling your potential Godhood on earth as much as is possible. You are bringing God to earth, insofar as you are able, through the expression of your individuality in a constructive way.

I understand individuality is a gift beginning with incarnate life, and yet the angels must be individual. Please clarify.

Your confusion comes from the fact that you are not recognizing that individuality is a fact; throughout the universes, every miniscule bit of life is totally individual.

What then is peculiar to incarnate life?

The difference is not defined by life in the incarnate world. As life ascends in degrees of consciousness, individuality is no longer fixed but capable of infinite development. The great yearning for free will resulted from a recognition of this possibility. The granting of free will was also a recognition of this — even though it entailed the risk of negative as well as positive development. This is truly the great adventure that was embarked upon, and that can be completed successfully only if you understand it is a long journey, each stage of which must advance you on your way.

The dangers of the present situation were seen as necessary to the solution. As the nature of Deterrent Force becomes clear, human beings will use their own free will to choose God's Will over self-will. This will reestablish their bond to the world from which they have become estranged.

Final Distillation

Responsibility

I will close this conversation with a distillation of what we have been discussing.

This communication has been about you as part of Deterrent Force contributing to evil. You are to accept responsibility for what is going on in the world, as well as for alleviating the ills that you have caused. Your effort must be first with yourself, and secondarily with those upon whom you have influence. Try to remember that time is the medium through which an incarnation is brought about. If you allow time to slip away from you, you are losing a portion of your incarnation that can never be retrieved. Every incarnation is a privilege and a responsibility, and you need to realize that now is the time to come to grips with your problems if God's Will is to be done. Each priceless moment counts, and there must be an end to waste. Hopelessness can be met by the knowledge of our spiritual equipment and its use. There is no way the evil in the world will disappear except through the efforts of people to align themselves with God so effectively that He will be present on earth through them. It is the process of becoming good or becoming evil that is of paramount importance. Society must be won back, one by one, each of us proceeding in our own way.

When Christ asked us to pray "Thy kingdom come. Thy Will be done in earth, as it is in Heaven," He was specifying that this realization was necessary for the completion of God's Will for every soul. Each of you must accept responsibility to accomplish this on earth.

Evil

Evil is the result of what human beings have done, but human beings have become the victims of their own creation.

We speak of evil as that which results from the intention of human beings through the use of Deterrent Force. Those, who feel themselves masters over all, who use self-will as a means of achieving their desires, become in the process one with the instrument that enables them to accomplish their ends. In so doing, they identify with the instrument they have chosen — Deterrent force — and in the process they become elements of Deterrent Force itself. Instead of having mastery over it; they are victimized by it, and the result of their efforts has a devastating effect on all concerned. It is necessary to understand that the use of such a powerful force can create, through the Law of parallels, a far greater outcome than was originally desired or intended. If you play with matches, you will inevitably get burned. So it is with the use of Deterrent Force. We had better know that continued association with such a harmful element can bring results that are indeed evil.

On the other hand, the ramifications of evil can be alleviated in those who cross its path by their reactions to it. However, the perpetrators don't get off so easily. The continuing use of Deterrent Force is so overpowering to the moral and spiritual elements of their beings that they end up aligned with the Forces of Darkness, victimized by the will they have projected upon others. Responding to the help that is always available is very difficult under these pressures, but until they do, they are lost souls, alienated from the Will of God.

Love

The essence of truth is the Love of God. Through love, truth is revealed. To deter truth is to deter God's Love and thereby create a vacuum into which evil can enter. However, we cannot separate ourselves truly from the Love of God. Humanity is the result of God's desire. In spite of how we behave, we are loved and are given the opportunity, through Grace, to change at will. We are tolerated, forgiven, protected, fed, nourished, clothed, and taught to an endless degree. Somehow or other God's Will will be done. No matter how long it is deterred by man's attraction to evil. God's Will will be done. This is our underlying premise. We have considered what deters God's Love and God's Will and the ways in which we are all a part of it, the consequences for us and the plan for our salvation. The outcome is up to us.

In order to take the fate of the world seriously, you must understand the seriousness of your own fate. The implications of immortality are to be taken to heart. Life, incarnate or discarnate does not exist in a vacuum. It is part of a larger reality. The intention of this teaching is to help you understand that reality, and to absorb the meaning of God's Love for you.

Faith

What you do is dependent upon what you think. What you think is colored by what you believe. What you believe is crucial to your development. By responding to events constructively, you are acting upon your belief, as well as your faith in God's goodness and His concern for your welfare. You recognize that all circumstances and events, no matter how they may appear, are for your good, but that the good derived from each event depends upon your reaction to it. Because you have faith in God's Love and God's Will and the rectitude of moral law, you know that there is some element of growth to be gleaned from the lessons being taught at every turn. Through faith you learn just how dependent you are on God's Love to help you in this struggle with yourself. By believing that there are indeed no accidents, and that all events are purposeful, you are obeying the Will of God and assuming your rightful place in the struggle against evil.